BLEEDING STONE

BLEEDING STONE

BRIAN YAPKO

A REBEL SATORI IMPRINT
New Orleans & New York

Published in the United States of America by
Queer Space
A Rebel Satori Imprint
www.rebelsatoripress.com

Book design: Sven Davisson

Paperback ISBN: 978-1-60864-290-8
Ebook ISBN: 978-1-60864-272-4

Library of Congress Control Number: 2023945003

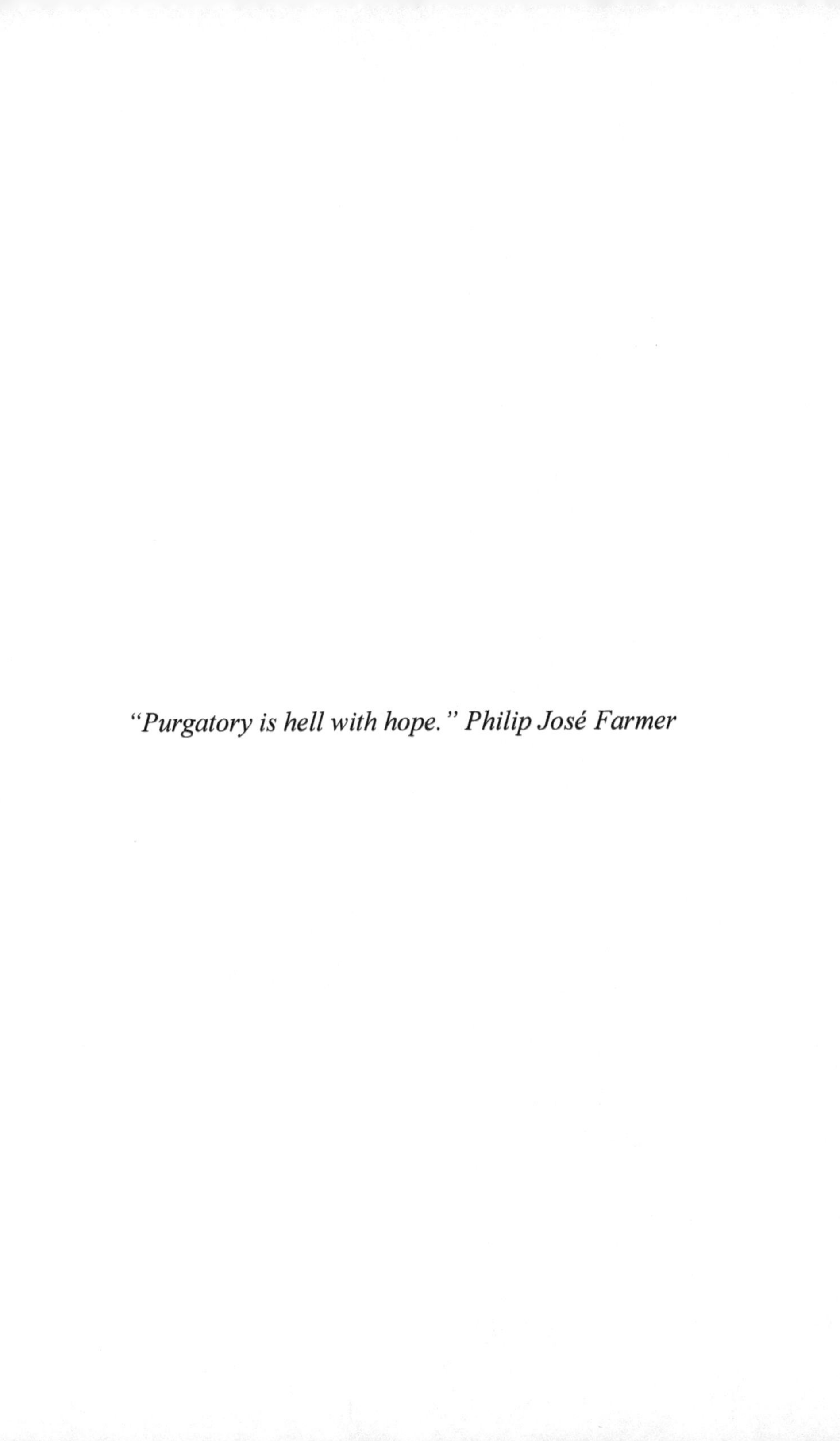

"Purgatory is hell with hope." Philip José Farmer

CONTENTS

PROLOGUE: THE DREAM OF THE JAGUAR

I just remembered the dream that I had all those years ago.

I was in that wretched run-down studio apartment in Hollywood. I was drifting off to sleep in the second-hand bed I frequently shared with my lover, Pedro. I was spooning him, my bare flesh connecting with his in half-a-dozen places from calf to shoulder. My calloused hand pulled his belly into me as if we could become one being with four arms, four legs and two heads. Pedro and I had made love for hours that night. We had also drunk too much tequila and I was now lost somewhere between sedated consciousness and a dream state. My head swam in the jungle darkness of the night as the neon sign on Yucca flashed the word "Girl, Girls, Girls" outside my window.

I rolled Pedro over and placed my lips against his, our mustaches rubbing together. I closed my eyes and deep-kissed him, my hands exploring all over his body. I heard him moan, then purr like a cat. My hand creeped upward, groin to belly. But when I reached his chest, I became terrified. Something was very wrong! Instead of warm flesh I felt only cold, unyielding metal. The purring sound became a feral growl. My eyes flew open and tight in my embrace was one of the jaguars of Tikal, attendant to the Mayan gods of my ancestors.

Pedro's eyes burned red, he snarled viciously and began to wrestle with me. His claws mauled at my chest and drew blood. In desperation,

I yelled for help calling out the strange name Buluc Chabtan, the Mayan god of war. I begged this god to make Pedro normal again, to give him back his heart, his humanity. *What was I willing to do in exchange?* he asked me. *Anything,* I answered. But the war god betrayed me. Never would I have guessed that Buluc Chabtan would call to Ah Puch, the most dreaded deity in the Mayan pantheon, the blood-thirsty god of death. Ah Puch materialized to the sound of frantic, ghostly whispers, the distant beat of drums and with blood dripping from his lips. He leered and reached for me with claw-like hands. When he grabbed my shoulder all of my skin from head to toe began to turn indigo blue. Then all three of these supernatural beings tried to pin me down. Naked and sweating, I wrestled with each of them, the war god, the death god and the jaguar. I panted and screamed, "Pedro, Pedro, help me! Come back!"

And suddenly he did! My Pedro, now perfectly normal, shook me awake and said that I had been screaming in my sleep. My heart was beating wildly. I stared at him as if I couldn't get enough of the sight of him. I reached out and placed my hand on his chest. My hand was a normal flesh tone again. And under the smooth skin of his chest I felt the steady heartbeat of the one man who actually loved me even though I surely did not deserve it.

Pedro rubbed my back until my breathing returned to normal. He got out of bed and brought me some water. Tenderly caressing my stubbled cheek, he told me to go back to sleep. We both laid down on the bed but now our positions were reversed with him spooning me. He kissed me on the neck. I felt his groin rub up against me, not hard with lust but soft with easy familiarity. *Ay.* Pedro and I were two scarred men loving each other in a rickety bed in a poor tenement building in the worst section of Hollywood.

And I would give every last dollar of my considerable wealth to be back with him in that rat-infested hell-hole.

And there's something else I just remembered: Buluc Chabtan and Ah Puch! When I had this nightmare, I had no idea that these Mayan gods even existed, let alone what their names were! How on Earth did these names come to me? Peculiar, no?

CHAPTER 1: PEDRO LUNA

So, *amigos*, is this a love story or a horror story? It is both. It is neither. Whatever you end up deciding, be warned that it has been penned by someone who is not a nice man. I confess that to you at the start. Nevertheless, even men who are not nice may have stories which deserve to be told.

Just know this, *mis amigos*: Life is strange. Stranger than anything you'll find on the decadent streets of Hollywood. Stranger than the fantasy stories I pitch to film studio executives who know nothing of life beyond the walls of their bougainvillea-framed Beverly Hills mansions. They think they know important things because of what they hear when they gather for their three -martini power lunches at chic restaurants on Rodeo Drive before hitting the golf course. Trust me. They do not.

You want to know the height of irony? They have me working on a fantasy project right now for Destiny Studios – unoriginal rubbish about treasure hunters who are cursed when they steal a sacred object. When they sent me the contract to write this trash all I could do was laugh! Well, I signed the contract. But I don't intend to meet their deadline. Shoot me – for all the good that'll do. I'm putting the Destiny screenplay aside. I need to record my own life once and for all. You see, I'm weighing whether or not to go back to Tikal.

Guatemala is calling me. The time has come. I want to bring this real-life story to a head.

But before I go, I need you to know what happened to me – the hell I invited into my life.

I had my reasons. Was it worth it? *Amigos*, once I am finished sharing my story you will tell me.

I want to start with something that happened two weeks before Tikal. The memory still haunts me. Pedro and I were at sea on the *Doña Maria*. I'd been drinking heavily and was thinking long and hard about how sexy my Pedro looked wearing a pair of boxer briefs and nothing else. He aroused me but the poor man was seasick. His left hand was pressed against his flat belly. I pulled at his hand to kiss him. He said now was a bad time. In my frustration I then said something very stupid. With his right hand he slapped my face. Then he called me a heartless bastard.

He said it in Spanish. "*Cabrón sin corazón.*"

Heartless. *Ay, amigos*, being called "heartless" has dogged me my whole life, long before Pedro. Catrina said it to me when I was ten and I scared off one of her married lovers. Later on, Mr. Simms, my gym teacher, said it when I refused to recant my description of his uninvited gropings. After that, it was Sister Bertha. And later still, Lydia, that sweet *chica* who I dumped when I met a handsome, struggling actor named Ramon. There were others. Many others. *Heartless.* Everyone who has ever cared about me said it. You get called something often enough you start to believe it, no?

But when Pedro said it, it really stung. I never cared about people much my whole life – not family, not friends. But him I cared about. Pedro Luna, *mi amor*. We argued in our steerage cabin at the waterline of the ship while the *Doña Maria* rocked back and forth. We were in a squall somewhere off the coast of Mexico. We were headed for Guatemala. The radio was playing. Jazz, I think. It was a sad time for him. For me too. His sister, Magdalena, had recently died in childbirth, and *el niño* – the baby boy – just one week later.

Alright, *amigos*. The first of many disclosures. It's best I tell you now so that you are not later surprised by proof that I was once as much pig as I was a man. Pedro – handsome, bright-eyed Pedro – was my lover. But his sister, Magdalena, had also been my occasional lover. And the baby boy who had died was mine.

Pedro was fully aware that I had gotten his sister pregnant. And Magdalena was equally aware that although I loved her, I was *in* love with her younger brother. We were all very modern, no? In a way, that made it easier. As Magdalena lay dying from the complications of a difficult childbirth, she asked Pedro and me to be a family, to raise the boy who was both my son and his nephew. Unfortunately, *el niño* had a weak heart. You can imagine the rest. They're both buried in Golgotha Cemetery in East Los Angeles.

As Pedro and I now argued on the *Doña Maria*, it was two months later and he was still grieving the deaths of Magdalena and the child – especially the child. Well, so was I! But I tried to get him to see the positive. Pedro and I weren't married, after all. Pedro was anxious to be a parent, but I told him over and over that not having a child meant freedom! And although I was physically very capable of getting a woman pregnant again maybe I wasn't really father material.

For some reason, my raising these points didn't make him feel better. I wanted to relax him, so I pulled Pedro to me and started to massage his shoulders, begging him to snap out of it. He pulled away and swore at me. Then, *pendejo* that I am, I grabbed his hand from his ailing stomach and called him a nasty word invoking a very old profession.

That's when he slapped me and called me "heartless." He told me to go to hell – that I should just go on to Guatemala by myself. He'd disembark in Acapulco.

I regretted insulting him. Hell, I loved him. I should have told him so but I was drunk on illegal tequila. I passed out with the words "heartless bastard" ringing in my ears.

Do you want to know why Pedro came with me to Guatemala? It was simple. He loved me. He wanted to be wherever I was – especially after we'd been separated for so long. You see, I was finally back on the outside after spending three years in prison.

Discretion, please, regarding this prison disclosure, *amigos*. I confess to having a double life. Or maybe I should say I've had two dramatically different lives: the conscienceless, amoral smuggler who barely subsisted before Tikal – and the successful Hollywood writer and real estate investor who came afterwards. My prison term was a long time ago. No one knows about my checkered past either at the Writers Guild or at Sotheby's. On the other hand, nobody knows my real name, so who gives a damn?

Anyway, when I told Pedro I was going to El Cruce in the Guatemalan rainforest – that I had some family business I had to handle there – Pedro said he wanted to come. My first reaction was no. He was still too traumatized, and I was burned out. But after he wheedled me nonstop for two days, I shrugged. Why not? I began to fantasize about trudging through the jungle with him, stopping to rest under the canopy, making love under the stars.

Maybe you're wondering why I wanted to be with Pedro at all. Some people dismissed him as just a cheap *puto* from East L.A.. But never me. Don't laugh at me, *amigos*. I cared for him. Pedro was lithe. He had sexy brown eyes and full lips. He had a scar on his right cheek from a violent trick and another one from a razor blade across his left wrist which he refused to discuss. But those full lips spoke kindness, his touch sparked intense heat and the passionate joining of our bodies in the bedroom was one of the few consistent pleasures in my life. Yes, he was scarred. But to me he was handsome. Maybe he was just a male prostitute, but he was proud, too. He refused to be ashamed of his background. He never answered to "Pete" or *chico* or "boy." Believe it or not, he had dignity. If you expected him to respond, you called him Pedro. Period.

I never judged him because he sold himself. Who the hell was I? If Pedro turned tricks, it was because he had no other choice. Was I there to take care of him? No. I was stuck behind bars like the *estúpido* felon that I was. Did he ever judge me? No, *amigos*. He did not. I loved this man as much as a heartless bastard was capable of loving. I think what I was willing to endure in Tikal – and afterwards – proves that.

Pedro thought this trip to Guatemala would be fun, maybe even romantic. But I warned him. This would not be a pleasure cruise. It was business. Criminal business.

We were going to break a dozen laws by stealing Mayan artifacts.

More specifically, gold. You think that sounds a bit *loco*? Like this B-movie screenplay I'm working on? Well, get off your high horses. The gold I was after was real. Oh, *amigos*, you better believe it was real. Mayan gold – sacred – from the *Templo de los Muertos* in Tikal. The kind of treasure a man would risk death for.

Anyway, I have nothing to prove to you. Much of that gold is right here, ten feet from the desk I'm typing on, hidden in my safe. Where do you think the seed money came from for a poor *pendejo* like me to end up as a major player in California real estate?

But *amigos*, there's more to this story than Mayan gold. Let me get back to the beginning. You see, this is Pedro's story as much as my own. And Pedro used to hate it when I told things out of order.

CHAPTER 2: THEY CALL ME MUNDO

Let's start with the basics. My name – the real one you will never see or hear – is Edmundo Lopez. I've lived in Los Angeles most of my life. In my pre-Tikal days, they called me "Mundo." I'm half-Guatemalan and half-unknown. "Unknown" because my so-called mother slept around a lot with men she never saw a second time.

Some might describe me as a lean, handsome *hombre* – black hair, brown eyes with an unusual sparkle, maybe even a sexy smile. Once when Pedro was lying next to me after a night of unbridled love making he whispered into my ear that I was as handsome as the devil. But let's not go down that road. Pedro's name is tattooed on my arm. I used to have *el Sagrado Corazón* – the Sacred Heart – on my chest but scarring has obscured it. I have a third tattoo on my inner thigh next to *mis privadas* – a scorpion. In the years when we enjoyed each other's bodies, Pedro liked to kiss that tattoo – for luck, he said – before pressing his lips to the excitement he invariably inspired. With the exception of my strange uncle, Pedro was the last human being to see that little scorpion. That was on the night before we reached Tikal. Yep, *amigos*. It's been a long time.

Back before Tikal, I was dirt poor. Now I live in a nice condominium off of Sunset Boulevard in the hills above West Hollywood. Alright, it's more than nice. I live in the penthouse. It's 6,000 square feet and has stunning views of L.A., Beverly Hills and the Hollywood sign. Zillow says it's worth about $6,000,000. It's filled with priceless antiques from Europe, paintings by the best artists of the 20th Century and, of course, archaeological treasures from Mexico, Guatemala and Honduras.

I own many other pieces of real estate besides the condominium. Between my real estate investments, my pseudonymed screenwriting gigs and the sacred Mayan gold hidden in my safe, this once poor *chico* from the streets has become a frighteningly wealthy – and reclusive – man.

As for family, well they pretty much count for *nada*. My dead so-called mother was from El Cruce, Guatemala. I've already told you about my anonymous father. When I look in the mirror, I can guess that he was extremely good looking, but I have to assume he's dead now too. I have no brothers or sisters. The only relative I've ever known other than my mother was my strange Uncle Carlos in El Cruce, but – after Tikal – who knows what the hell happened to him? I call him "strange" because... well, you'll find out soon enough.

My so-called mother's name was Catrina. This whole story exists because of her. She gave me life. Then she destroyed it. You know something, *amigos?* I can't bring myself to call that witch either *mother* or *madre*. From here on out, she's just Catrina. Towards the end, she was a woman whose dark beauty had faded decades ago from too many cigarettes, too much gin and too many men. She was long past her prime, but you'd never know it from the way she dressed in tight, loud clothes.

This is the woman who left me alone in a rickety apartment to cook and clean for a week by myself while she went on a pleasure jaunt to Catalina with some gambler. I was nine years old at the time. This is the woman who sent me out into the streets crying as she made me beg strangers on the street for money to help pay for a bottle of liquor she had smashed on the floor while she was drunk. I was eleven. This is the woman who went out of her way to tell every girl or guy I ever cared about that I was heartless, that I should never have been born, that I'd never amount to anything. Charming, huh? Catrina. Like those dressed up female skeletons you see on the *Dia de los Muertos*.

A few months before Pedro and I went to Tikal, Catrina was still alive but very sick with cancer of the breast. It had come upon her unexpectedly and, negligent as she was, she didn't have it treated until it was too late. Before she died, she decided to tell me the secret she'd kept for almost forty years. She and her younger brother, Carlos – 13 and 10 years old back then – had run away from home and ended up many miles away, lost among the ruins of Tikal.

I've mentioned Tikal a few times so far. You've heard of it, no? A truly magnificent Mayan city which reached its peak around 800 A.D. and was then mysteriously abandoned. The ruins weren't rediscovered until the 19th Century.

Anyway, Catrina whispered to me that she and Carlos had discovered gold in Tikal's *Templo de los Muertos* – a giant pyramid shaped building, she said, with many mysteries. Yes, they found gold but stole none of it. This made no sense to me. They were dirt-poor farmers. A pocket full of gold could have set them up for life! But Catrina said that they were "afraid to offend the gods." Yeah, right. That struck me as pretty funny coming from someone whose hypocrisy allowed her to send me to parochial school when she never set foot in a church the entire time I knew her.

In hindsight, there are things in her story that just don't add up. How do a couple of children "run away" 75 miles or so through the thick Guatemalan jungle and just happen to find the most magnificent of all Mayan ruins? How do they find the entrance into the one temple that houses the Mayan treasury? How do they learn the secret of entry into that treasury? *Amigos*, there is much to this story that she never told me. If only she were one of my voices and I could ask her...

Forgive the digression. All I knew at the time were the half-truths that witch told me.

So, when she was on her deathbed Catrina told me how rotten she felt for not giving me a good life. She said she realized that her careless choices might have led to my criminal lifestyle. What could I say to that? She was an uncaring *puta*! I had no father. As far back as I could remember Catrina had bounced from shiftless lover to shiftless lover – usually married – not one of whom ever took any interest in her boy. So yeah. The terrible upbringing she gave me factored large in leading me into an incautious life of petty crime.

Catrina said she had a way to make up for being a bad mother. This secret treasure consisting of gold and jade in Tikal "would set all things right." She wanted me to meet her brother, Carlos, in El Cruce. Uncle Carlos and I would find the treasure, split it 50:50 and I could start my life over. Catrina said it was an expedition that required bravery, but if I loved gold I'd find enough to make me rich. She repeated that loaded phrase: "It would set all things right."

There was a glitch. The only contact she had with Carlos was by mail. She said there was no other way. In El Cruce there was no electricity. It was completely off the grid. Only old-fashioned mail would get there. And although she wrote to him regularly, he hadn't responded in three years.

"Jeez!" I said. "What if he's dead?"

'*Ay*, Mundo. That *cabrón* will never die." Her cackle turned into a hacking cough

The last thing I asked her was "What about your childhood worry?

Of offending the gods?

Her face contorted into a grim smiling skull with garish lipstick still adorning those profane lips. "To hell with them," Then she died. I wish I could say I cried, but I didn't. Yeah, I know. Heartless me.

But not completely heartless. My pulse raced when I thought about Mayan gold. I didn't need a king's ransom. Just enough to get me started. I may have been a petty smuggler, but I was pretty smart, you know? I always wanted to go legit. I just needed a chance. I could use the gold as seed money to invest in stock – maybe buy an apartment building in Hollywood. Or, hell. Why not Beverly Hills? Plus, I had this secret dream of becoming a writer. I'd kept a journal ever since I was a boy. Before I was a heartless criminal, I was a sensitive young *hombre*. I wrote stories. I kept the journal, with all of my secrets and all of my fantasies, hidden under my bed. Even into my twenties, I liked to write stories. I never had the confidence to try to sell them, but I always thought *maybe... just maybe...*

Listen, *amigos*. Before we get to Tikal, there's one last thing about me that you need to know. The details about why I went to prison. You see, when Catrina died, I'd been out of Folsom for six months and was still kind of lost. So, I was grateful that Catrina finally came through for me with this Tikal treasure hunt. It was a project I could get behind.

What I forgot was how much Catrina resented me. It never occurred to me that she wanted revenge for something bad that I had done. Like I said, I was a smuggler who imported illegal product from Mexico. A guy's gotta eat, no? But I never got into trouble with the law until this last time when I messed up my first and only armed robbery. Why would I rob someone? I was desperate. I had a *jefe* that I had to answer to. If I didn't come up with my weekly payout to *El Pirata* I was going to end up dead.

So, my one and only armed robbery ended in disaster. The pawn shop owner was Jose Garza – a name I can never forget. He and his family lived over the shop. It was the middle of the night. Garza heard me break in and tried to stop me. I tried to be a tough guy and brandished my knife. You know what he did next? The bastard had a heart attack and fell down the stairs! He was in the process of yelling at me to leave the premises and warning me that he had a gun when I heard him gasp. He called out words I didn't recognize (I realized much later they were the names Buluc Chabtan and Ah Puch.) Then he clutched at his chest and toppled down the stairs. I actually tried to save him from breaking his neck. I jumped in front of him to stop his fall and the knife I was brandishing ended up lodged in my thigh. It didn't matter. Nothing could have saved him. *Nada.* By the time he reached the bottom of the stairs, he was dead. I howled in pain, and I remember his wife screaming, children crying and only a few minutes later the cops were there. They found me in terrible pain, bleeding like a stuck pig with a fat dead man pinned on top of me.

Believe it or not, I didn't get charged for his death. It wasn't murder if I didn't intend it, right? Garza had a heart attack fair and square. At least that's what everybody thought. That's what the autopsy said and there was no way for the D.A. to argue otherwise. As for Garza's wife – an improbably pretty woman named Teresa – I think maybe she was happy he was gone. He had been two-timing her. So, the armed robbery/voluntary manslaughter charges were reduced to one count of breaking and entering and one count of burglary. Despite my reckless lifestyle, this was the first felony I was ever charged with so my public defender was able to plea bargain the charges into a three year sentence.

As for Catrina – I thought she would never forgive me. How the hell was I supposed to know that Jose Garza was her lover? And, true to her pattern, a married one at that. And how was I supposed to know that Jose Garza was from Guatemala just like her? That they had known each other in El Cruce? And, most importantly, how was I to know that Garza had some mysterious ties to Tikal – that his death would cause fall-out on a scale I could never have imagined?

Catrina never forgave me for his death. When I showed her the knife scar in my thigh from where I tried to save her married lover, she just spat on the floor. She called me heartless and said I had no idea what consequences would result from this death. *Amigos*, I had no idea what she meant. What could possibly be so important about this fat Guatemalan pawnshop owner?

Catrina never once visited me in prison. She came down with cancer just about that time, but that's not why she never came to see me. It was because she hated me. All my life I'd been nothing but a burden to her. I had interfered with her freedom, her drinking, her own petty cons and her sordid love affairs. Finally, I had caused the death of a man she had secretly cared for (or so she said) and who she had apparently pinned her financial future on.

So, from her deathbed Catrina wanted vengeance. And – I didn't know it at the time – Jose Garza had a debt to be paid. A heavy debt. Someone had to make good on it. That's why she lured me to Guatemala with this story of Mayan gold. She really knew how to get to me.

The jade she mentioned never captured my imagination. But gold? Ah, glittering, meltable, fungible gold. What could be closer to the nonexistent heart of a petty thief and accidental murderer?

CHAPTER 3: THE DOÑA MARIA

One week after Catrina's death I wrote to her brother, my Uncle Carlos. I didn't hear back from him for over a month but attributed that to the slow mail service into rural Guatemala. When I did finally hear from him it was a very cold, abrupt letter – not one word of condolence for my mother's death. All he said was, to paraphrase: he had heard about me from Catrina. Yes, I should come. A visit to the temples of Tikal was overdue. It would set all things right.

Alright, so Carlos wasn't a warm, fuzzy guy. What mattered was that he would lead me to the ancient treasure, right? I looked at pictures of Mayan discoveries at the library. Jade masks, gold implements, gold and jade bracelets, gold carvings. Gold... I was becoming obsessed with it. After a life that had been full of misery and had mostly gone wrong I had decided that this Mayan gold was my birthright – to make up for all the things Catrina had cheated me out of.

Ay, amigos... I already told you about Pedro and how he wanted to come along on this trip. But I haven't told you how deeply Pedro wanted us to be a family, him, me and the boy Magdalena died giving life to. The son who I had fathered. She had given him to Pedro and me to raise as our son. We followed Magdalena's last wishes and named him Roberto. But he had a congenital heart defect. I only ever held him in my arms for a few minutes and only while wearing a surgical mask in the presence of nurses. He only lived a week. If he hadn't had that flaw in his heart, well... he would have been kind, smart, honest, successful – everything I wasn't. Imagine me a father! Don't you dare laugh at me, *amigos*. I still get choked up thinking about it.

Pedro spent a long time mourning Magdalena and Roberto. He cried often in those first weeks. So did I at first. But you probably know me well enough by now to see that I bounce back. Pedro didn't. For a while he became a ghost man. Even though he and I were together, he felt like he had nothing to live for. I kissed him. I bought him things. *Nada.* I was starting to feel like he was beyond help. So, when Pedro said he wanted to come with me to Guatemala, how could I say no? Life had to start over somehow. Maybe we could recapture something. Look, I admit that I've been a foul, profane *hombre* for much of my life, but I've always believed in something that manages our lives. Well, I prayed to that something before beginning this journey. I prayed I would get all the gold that I deserved. And I prayed that Pedro would get his life back. *Amigos*, you'll decide how fairly my prayers were answered.

After a month of preparation (forging documents and liquidating assets takes time, *amigos*) Pedro and I boarded the *Doña Maria* out of Long Beach. Neither of us had anything to leave behind. No families, no jobs to speak of, and no homes other than my pathetic little studio apartment and the rat-infested hotel rooms Pedro rented by the week. Frankly, if we disappeared, no one would ever know the difference. Pedro, at least, had a relative – his aunt Josefina in Florida. With Magdalena dead, she was his only living relative. As for me, I had nobody. Literally, nobody other than my mother's brother in El Cruce. That was okay. Maybe if we found this Mayan treasure I could forge a new identity. Pedro and I could start over. If it made Pedro happy, we could even adopt a kid, build a family. I could stop trying to scrape a living distributing smuggled goods and invest my gold into something legitimate that I could turn into a real money-maker. I was going to be Somebody if it killed me.

We left October 15th. The *Doña Maria* was a Chilean freighter headed for Valparaiso which offered extra cabin space to paying passengers. When you have no money you do it on the cheap, no? Plus we were able to negotiate a discount because we knew one of the officers well enough to blackmail his cooperation. Victor was a real *macho* who was one of Pedro's regular tricks. He had a wife who knew nothing. He wanted to keep it that way.

The *Doña Maria* had ports of call in San Diego, Mazatlan, and then Puerto San José in Guatemala, so it worked out perfectly. I was excited to finally be traveling someplace new. The only travel I had ever done in my life up to then was back and forth between L.A. and Tijuana. Now I would see grand things. Jungles! Ruins! I had amazing dreams about the pyramids of the Maya in Central America. Vivid dreams involving jaguars and the quetzal bird. And sometimes I had nightmares which caused me to wake up moaning in a cold sweat.

This was my first time on a ship at sea. *Amigos*, it was better than anything I could have expected! I took to it right away. Blue skies, rolling waves leading to forever, salt in your face, air so fresh you could eat it and keep wanting more. On the Pacific Ocean there was freedom and infinite possibility – and nothing to make a man feel trapped. But not for Pedro. He was still sad. He would crack a smile once in awhile like the time we were on deck and we saw a whale breach the surface and spout. But he spent most of the voyage either seasick or else staring out at the endless ocean. The sea air made me feel robust. The rolling waves for me were a sensual experience. But for Pedro it was anything but.

Midway through the trip was that "heartless bastard" incident I've already told you about. Like I said, it still haunts me. Pedro would have been within his rights to leave the ship and head back to L.A. But he didn't. I'm sorry he didn't. I'm so grateful that he didn't.

CHAPTER 4:
GUATEMALA

After a few more days we arrived in Puerto San José. Talk about culture shock! Guatemala was nothing like L.A.! Coconuts, monkeys, ramshackle houses made out of stray pieces of plywood and corrugated iron. Poverty, barefoot people. Donkeys and mosquitos! Frequent rain and a humid heat that just hits you in the face and makes you spit sweat.

Once off the ship we were truly on our own. My Spanish was good since I'd grown up with Catrina speaking it at home. Pedro's mother was also Guatemalan so he was equally at home in either language just as Magdalena had been. Still, the language of Guatemala was different from California Spanish somehow and, tough as I am, I felt like a stranger in a strange land.

And then a strange thing happened. We were wandering about the *Plaza de Armas* looking for a place to lodge. There was an old lady who was selling blankets and kept staring at Pedro as if she knew him. Before we even noticed, she came up to him and threw a Mayan cloth over his shoulders while she hummed and then said some words in a dialect neither of us could understand. We said that we didn't want to buy anything. The old lady responded with a toothless smile. The gift was simply because he was "a handsome señor." Pedro lit up. It was the first time I'd seen him really smile in months. Then she seemed to notice me for the first time. Her face became grim, she crossed herself and then went back to her stall. I said nothing but couldn't help wondering what her reaction meant.

From Puerto San José it was another 400 miles inland to El Cruce, near the Mexican border on the southern edge of the Yucatan peninsula. We had to plan a long trek through volcano country. There were no trains or planes and I sure as hell wasn't getting on one of those chicken buses. Once we found lodging near the port, we went for drinks at a local cantina to figure out how to get up north. We listened to a sad-looking woman strumming a guitar and drank two or three tequila shots. Finally, we ended up meeting a coffee merchant who was trying to sell his used Ford. It wasn't in bad shape and I was able to bargain him down to the equivalent of 100 U.S. dollars. That car turned out to be surprisingly reliable.

We stayed in Puerto San José mapping out our route and preparing for the drive. We filled up with gas, including some extra containers. We bought food for the car and then we were off! The roads were muddy, and we got lost more than once. It took us three days to get to El Cruce. We slept in ramshackle inns two of those nights and the Ford on the third night but eventually we made it.

Amigos, let me tell you about El Cruce. Remote, rustic – but In a way it had its own charm. Its roads were unpaved and it was situated on a muddy lake called Peten Itza, surrounded by the dense Guatemalan rainforest with steep volcanoes in the distance. Talk about stepping into the past! This was a village of only a few hundred people with ramshackle houses, a tiny church with a straw roof and dirt roads. It was like traveling back to the early 1800s. The villagers got water from a community well. There was no electricity. Chickens and the occasional monkey roamed around at will. People kept goats, caught wild turkeys and grew *frijoles* and corn. This little pueblo was where my ancestors came from – at least on my mother's side. As I looked at the faces of the people, they looked familiar – like they could have been my cousins. And perhaps they were! I was vaguely excited to see the ancestral home but, to be honest, I was too much of a city boy to want to stay there. Pedro, on the other hand, had the perspective of a true romantic. He'd had enough of neon lights, the sounds of traffic, sirens blaring, litter and empty beer bottles in dark alleys. Pedro thought El Cruce was beautiful. In fact, once we had parked over in the plaza and got out of the car, he had trouble controlling his tears. I was baffled at the time, but in hindsight I think I understand why. But let me not get ahead of myself.

El Cruce could boast of several horses and burros, but not many cars. Certainly, there were no strangers, so when Pedro and I arrived we created quite a stir. I hoped that we'd get a warm welcome but instead people were suspicious. One man – I think he was the mayor – demanded to know who we were. What was I going to say? *"Buenos Dias,* I'm the man who killed Jose Garza from your village and this is my homosexual lover and, by the way, we're here to pillage Mayan gold?" No, the smartest thing to do was simply state that we were relatives of Carlos Lopez visiting from *Los Estados Unidos* and that we were interested in archaeology. I said nothing about Catrina and certainly nothing about Jose Garza.

The town leader nodded seriously. He gave me directions to the house my Uncle Carlos lived in. It was on the edge of town near the lake and adjacent to some bean fields. There was only a dirt road to get there, and it was impassably muddy so we left the car on the side of the *mercado* and walked.

Once we got to the edge of town it was easy enough to find my *Tío* Carlos. We called out to two shirtless men who were digging a drainage ditch. They pointed him out on the other side of the ditch. He was the *hombre* having a siesta in a hammock slung in front of a little house made of wood with a corrugated iron roof. From the ramshackle state of affairs, it seemed probable that he lived alone. There was no evidence of a wife or kids. Despite the oppressive heat, he was wearing blue jeans, a long-sleeved shirt, Panama hat and dark sunglasses – a uniform which never varied the whole time I knew him.

I called out to him. "Are you Carlos Lopez?"

His head lifted from the hammock, those dark sunglasses making the man's reaction to us inscrutable.

When I called out to him a second time Carlos got up slowly, stretched like a cat, removed the hat and shades and stared at us like we were intruders. That's when I thought someone had made a mistake. This man was far too young to be the brother my mother had told me about!

See, Catrina had me when she was young, right? When she died, she was only 51. Well, the math said that Carlos had to be 48 or so. But he looked almost the same age as me – I had just turned 31 on the ship from L.A. If you saw us standing together he could have been my cousin or my brother instead of my uncle. Maybe there was something to be said for the fresh air and the wild turkeys, eh?

But there was something else. Carlos was handsome in a way that I found disturbing. When he removed his shades, his eyes glittered with arrogance. I felt like he could see right through me. I had known *hombres* like this before – good-looking men, straight and gay alike, who would come-on to you, touch your shoulder maybe, and then mock you when you responded to their attention. But even if Carlos hadn't been my uncle, I would never have wanted him. There was something about him that my intuition warned me to stay clear of. I didn't like the way he looked at Pedro. More importantly, I really didn't like the way

Pedro looked at Carlos. I understood, of course. I have to admit that my too-young uncle was a handsome, swarthy *hombre*. So why wasn't he married? I had to wonder if he was gay but my usually-reliable gaydar said it wasn't probable. More likely he was divorced, a widower, or just such a narcissist that couldn't give a damn about anyone but himself. You know *amigos*, I have to laugh. Despite all that has happened after meeting that lousy bastard, I still don't know the answer.

After studying us for us a full minute, Carlos tossed his hat on the hammock and put his sunglasses back on. "I know who you are," he said in perfect English and without smiling. Then he switched to Spanish. "*Si, estoy Carlos. Su tio. Bienvenida al infierno.*" Welcome to hell."

Not your typical welcome, eh *amigos*? Like his abrupt letter, Carlos was cold when we met. Now I found out why. He may not have written to my mother very often, but Catrina wrote to him regularly. He knew all about me. He knew about my being in prison and why. Most importantly, he knew that the victim of the crime I was put away for was Jose Garza, the man who died of a heart attack but who she blamed me for killing.

When I held out my hand Carlos refused to shake it. Instead, this too young uncle said "Edmundo Lopez, don't expect me to like you even if you are my nephew. If my sister said you're a heartless *pendejo*, then to me you're a heartless *pendejo*. I want you to know something else. Jose Garza was a good friend of mine. His death creates a big hole."

Jeez. Garza again. Would the vindictive ghost of the pawn shop owner ever let me be? I retrieved the hand "Uncle" Carlos had refused to shake. "There's more to it than you can possibly understand, Carlos." I couldn't bring myself to call this strange, scowling man "*tio.*"

He walked up to me and stood in my personal space with his face so close to mine we breathed the same air. With those sunglasses on he looked like a giant insect. "This expedition, *nephew*... It's what my sister wanted. It will set things right. If you want gold so much that you were willing to travel here by ship and across all of Guatemala, then you will get your gold. *Sí*, there will be much satisfaction. But we are not destined to be *amigos*, you and I. This is strictly business."

I balled my hands into fists, but this arrogant, disrespectful *hombre* held the key to my future. I wanted to tell him about how loose his cheap sister had been, what kind of horrible mother she was, but I just forced myself to shrug. He loved her, not me. And not everyone has a warm, supportive family, do they?

I dreaded the abuse that my strange Uncle Carlos might inflict on Pedro, but to my surprise, Carlos greeted him politely. Maybe too politely. After treating me like dirt, I was shocked to see him study Pedro's face for a moment, nod slightly, take Pedro's hand and then bow low like gentlemen did with lovely *señoritas* in the old days. I confess that the strangely reverent expression on Carlos' face when he took my Pedro's hand made me jealous. But then Carlos abruptly released Pedro's hand as he assumed a sharp tone.

"The two of you are a homosexual couple?" Pedro nodded, surprised by the directness of the question. "So what if we are?" I said. I was instantly defensive and ready to strike my fist against his jaw. But it wasn't necessary. Carlos shrugged, ran a finger across Pedro's cheek, and then addressed us both with an expression somewhere between a grimace and a leer. "I don't care what you *maricóns* do with each other. I know well how flesh may burn when it touches the skin of another. But what you do together – do not let me see it. Do not let me hear it."

"I don't think that's for you..." Pedro began.

"I set the rules!" Carlos bellowed. Then his eyes narrowed. "If you want me to help you, you will leave me out of it, *Piedra*." That was another odd thing. From that point on Carlos began to refer to Pedro as *La Piedra.* At first, I thought that was just a homophobic slur. Like calling a manly dude "Nancy." But apparently, I was wrong. Pedro later reminded me that it was simply Spanish for "the rock." Strange.

I wondered if he would offer us any hospitality at all. The noon sun was beating down on us and we were thirsty. As if he read my mind Carlos said, "son of my sister, you will lodge here." He nodded to Pedro. "Both of you."

He led us onto the front porch of his tiny house. I wondered if he was ever going to let us inside. Instead, he had us sit on a bench by the front door as he grabbed a hand-carved wooden stool. He excused himself for a moment and then returned with three *cervezas.* "Let us talk some more. Then we will go to your car and retrieve your bags and gear."

He asked us questions about our drive to El Cruce from the Pacific. We answered them. He also asked us personal questions about our work in Los Angeles. We had to lie. Was I supposed to tell him that I was a smuggler and that Pedro offered himself to men for money? Carlos acted as if he believed the lies we offered but I don't think he did. While she was alive, Catrina had a very busy pen.

There was a lull in the conversation as I tried to assess how much I could manipulate my mother's brother. I have always had a gift for getting what I wanted from people. But, as with the mother I could never influence, my charms never worked on Carlos. To the contrary. He gulped the last of his beer and then hit his hand on the nearby table unexpectedly. Looking at us appraisingly he contradicted his own stated rule that he wanted nothing to do with our sex lives. "So you are two grown men who make passion with each other?"

"Carlos, I thought that we agreed that what we do is none of your goddamned business" I said very calmly.

"This is none of my goddamned business" he repeated to himself. "Let me ask you this. You are going to sleep under my roof until we are ready for the journey to Tikal?"

"Well..."

He laughed softly. Then he stood from his little stool, came over to me and patted my cheek. "No, nephew *maricón*, I suppose this is not my business." He spit on his own cement floor, then gestured at Pedro. "I'm just curious what would make a good-looking *hombre*, a kindly man like *La Piedra* want to waste his life with a *pendejo* like you."

Every word that came out of Carlos' mouth made me want to strangle him. I'd broken bones for lesser insults in prison and yet my rotten uncle was shaming me in front of the man I loved – at least as much love as my heartlessness would allow. What was Carlos's angle? I didn't believe that Carlos was gay and jealous of our relationship. I can spot gay in five seconds. No, Carlos was mocking us and clearly trying to goad me into some type of explosion. Short of smashing his handsome face in, I had no clue how to react to my uncle's strange conversation.

Bless him, Pedro stood up for me. He told Carlos that he loved me, that even if I had made mistakes at least I was trying. Carlos asked Pedro point blank "Does this *pendejo* love you?" I answered for him and said of course I did. He waved a dismissive hand at me. "I was talking to *La Piedra*." Carlos turned back to him, the tone in his voice purely academic. "Can a man who has no heart really love?"

Pedro took my arm and firmly said, "Mundo loves me, *Sénior* Carlos. And I love him." Pedro had a heart of gold, he did. Well... you know what I mean.

Carlos looked me up and down like I was mule he was considering buying. "*Nosotros veremos*" he said. "We shall see. Just keep it clean when

I'm around. You will be in separate beds *en mi casa*. And I don't want to see any of this." he said, grabbing at his crotch for emphasis. He smiled a twisted smile, turned his back on us and, ignoring our startled reactions, disappeared around the side of the house towards the lake.

I exhaled and tasted blood in my mouth from biting my tongue into silence. What in hell had I gotten us into?

"Well, are you coming?" He was yelling at us to follow him. "¡Vamanos! I'm not going to collect your bags and gear by myself." And so we followed his shortcut back into town. Before we went to the car to retrieve our bags, we stopped at the tortilleria and had some freshly made tortillas with beans. I confess, *amigos*, the best I've ever had. Then he had us stop at the local *mercado* to get some food "if we didn't want to go hungry." He said he had very little to eat at his house. Then we went to where we had parked the Ford, retrieved our stuff and walked the quarter mile back to his house.

We stayed in El Cruce with my unpredictable, too-young uncle Carlos for three days as we prepared for the long trek. The interior of his house was nothing like the bland, whitewashed exterior. There was a living room painted green and red. It was filled with clay pots and figurines which would, no doubt, be of interest to an anthropologist or archaeologist. I asked him where he got all of these objects. He just shrugged, his words cryptic. "Where we live is over 2000 years old."

"And what about the paint?" I asked regarding the garish colors of his interior.

"They are to please the Mayan gods," he said with great seriousness.

"What gods?" I questioned skeptically.

He looked at me and shook his head as if he pitied my ignorance. "Buluc Chabtan and Ah Puch." Seeing my puzzled expression he said "They are two of the most powerful gods in the Mayan pantheon. And yet you have never heard of them?"

The names seemed to sound vaguely familiar – like a dream memory triggered by a real-life experience. But I certainly wasn't going to tell him that. I just shook my head. "Never heard of them."

"When we get to Tikal I will make sure that you learn all about them." He said this with a crooked smile and a hint of malice. Why must he turn everything into a power struggle? I ignored this and said for him to stop talking about his ancient myths. Pedro and I were hungry and we said so.

Carlos then showed us his kitchen. It was small and primitive with no refrigerator and only a wood-burning stove. Now I understood why he had us pick up some groceries. The only food in the *casa* were some bottles of warm beer, some dried pork, some fruit and a few ears of corn. He handed us some of the pork which I wolfed down along with a couple of tortillas. .

The *baño* was an outhouse a few feet from the adjacent lake. And the shower was a hose that he had set up near the porch in the back of the house. He had no conveniences or luxuries whatsoever. He might as well have lived in a treehouse.

Carlos' house also included two bedrooms, both of which were painted the same garish red and green as the living room. His room contained a king size bed too large for one man. The other, where Pedro and I slept, was furnished with two single beds as if intended for children. The set-up of this *casa* only made sense if Carlos had a wife and children. And yet he was alone. Curiosity finally got the better of me. On the second night at his house, when we were relaxing on his porch over *cervezas*, I caught him staring at Pedro. Instead of getting jealous, I decided to stir the pot a little and asked him very bluntly why a good-looking *hombre* like him wasn't married?

He clearly understood what I was getting at because I saw him stiffen. I had been about to ask if he, too, was a *maricón*, but he glared at me through his tinted glasses as if I had made an unforgivable trespass. Then he said, "Careful, *pendejo*. Some things are not your business." Then he went into the *casa* and brought out one of his Mayan statues – one with an exaggerated phallus – and asked if it got me and Pedro excited. I nearly smashed this ancient statue from his hand but realized that it might be worth a small fortune.

I told him to put the object down. He winked at Pedro and then looked back to me. "Alright, *pendejo*. Have it your way."

My uncle Carlos could goad me more than anyone I'd met since I was stuck in Folsom. I told him to stop calling me *pendejo*, which means dumbass, more or less. He looked at me silently for a moment. Without warning he then threw his beer bottle against a rock and it shattered into a hundred pieces. "Then don't expect me to talk to you," he said quietly. With that he entered the house and slammed the door behind him. Pedro said "wait" and started to rise to coax Carlos back outside, but I grabbed his arm and stopped him. I could only take so much crazy in my life.

And I was certain that Carlos was crazy. A loose cannon. As unpredictable and dangerous as any nut-case I had met in prison. But he happened to be a nut-case who knew how to get to the Mayan gold that my entire future was riding on. So, like I said to Pedro, for the duration of this expedition we just had to keep it light to keep from setting him off. As mysterious as he was, I would make a point of never asking my strange uncle any personal questions again.

Pedro said he was tired and was going to bed. He left me alone on the porch staring out at the black waters of the lake and the incredible array of stars that hung over this section of rural Guatemala. I stood up and walked to the lake. A voice shouted at me from the *casa*. "Watch out for crocodiles, *pendejo!*"

Ay, another magical moment ruined courtesy of Uncle Carlos. At this point, I was impatient to leave El Cruce and move on to the archaeological site we were going to plunder. The sooner Pedro and I were done with Guatemala the better. This place was too full of mysteries. And my crazy, too-young Uncle Carlos was the biggest, most dangerous of them all.

Ha, *amigos!* I have to laugh. At the time, I actually thought that Carlos took top billing on my list of threats. But, of course, that was before Tikal.

The preparations that Carlos needed to make were the cause for our delay. My uncle was a farmer. He had fields of corn and beans as well as chickens and goats. Since we were going to be gone for at least a week, he needed to make arrangements to have the animals tended and the crops protected from the birds. He hired a very somber teenage boy named Miguel to handle the farm duties. Miguel would also watch over his house and – for some extra coins – keep his eye on my hundred-dollar Ford. We had other preparations to make as well. We needed food supplies and other gear sufficient for a trek into uninhabited rainforest. While Carlos took care of the equipment that we needed, Pedro and I basically bought out half the inventory of the local *mercado*.

I had trouble wrapping my mind around having to hike all the way to Tikal when I had a car. I repeatedly urged Carlos to allow us to use it.

"No. For one thing, where are you to find petrol? For another thing, what happens if *el carro* breaks down?"

"How long will it take us to get to Tikal?" I countered.

"Four days on foot," he answered.

"A ridiculous waste of time. If we take the car we could be at Tikal in only a few hours."

"Your automobile is out of the question, *pendejo*. As it is, even on foot, we dare not take the main road. The *policia*, they patrol it. They'll ask questions. There are bandits as well who would gladly shoot you for your clothing let alone for a car. Do not ask me again."

I accepted this last answer even if I didn't like it. His explanation made perfect sense. Oh, I wasn't worried about the *banditos*. Prison had made me strong. There was very little that I feared on this Earth, and I even had some extra protection that neither Carlos nor Pedro knew about. No, it was his mention of the police that grabbed my attention. What we were planning to do was big-time illegal. Guatemala had strict laws regarding the theft of artifacts – especially jade and gold. Plus, strictly speaking, Pedro and I were in Guatemala illegally on forged papers. We did not dare come to the attention of any authorities. So, what should have been a drive of only a couple of hours to cover the 88 miles from El Cruce to Tikal, would now be a four day trek on foot with only Carlos's burro to help carry our supplies through the dense rainforest.

Pedro's eyes gleamed when we talked about this. He placed his hand on my arm. "How romantic this will be, Mundo! Don't you think?"

Carlos overheard this statement. "It will be many things, *La Piedra*," he said. "But romantic is not one of them."

CHAPTER 5: THROUGH THE RAINFOREST

We got our start early on a Sunday in late October. I believe it was the 26th. Carlos, Pedro, his burro and me. Before we left, Carlos had to give the strangely somber people of El Cruce a cover story to explain why he was guiding two strangers from America into the jungle. The whole time we were there he said nothing to any of the villagers about the fact that I was his nephew. He told them some nonsense about Pedro and me being butterfly collectors and paying him as a guide. From the skeptical faces of the villagers I doubt anyone believed Carlos but no one seemed interested in challenging him. He was too volatile.

A half hour into our long trek, after all remnants of civilization were behind us, I made a joke to Carlos about our missing church. It was Sunday, after all. He stopped the burro and pointed his finger at me. His tone was sharp. "What we're doing church has nothing to do with. Why should a heartless bastard like you care, *pendejo?*" That did it. Did he think I was an animal without feelings? Did he think I didn't believe in anything because of where I had been? I bashed my walking stick against a tree to make him look at me. I was getting sick and tired of the lack of respect this so-called uncle kept throwing at me. I exploded. I shouted that he better stop calling me *pendejo* or there'd be hell to pay.

At that, Carlos threw his supply bag to the ground at my feet and said I could damn well go on alone – "North is that way." He started to walk back towards El Cruce with the burro. After all Pedro and I had gone through to get this far, I now saw my financial future disappearing away with him.

Pedro shouted "Carlos, come back!" He stopped but did not turn around. I gritted my teeth. "Fine, *Uncle* Carlos. Treat me however you want. Call me whatever the hell you want." He turned around and looked at me through narrowed eyes. I made an exaggerated bow and said "*Pendejo* Lopez, at your service. But I warn you. Treat me like an animal and I may bare my teeth like an animal."

The smile he displayed had malice in it. He walked back to where Pedro and I were waiting, leading his burro. He handed Pedro the reins and continued to come towards me until he stood in my personal space, his face practically in mine just like on that first day we met him. He was very quiet and very menacing. "I will come with you for my sister's sake, *pendejo*. To make things right with Mayan treasure." He turned back to Pedro who he had taken a liking to. "And for the sake of *La Piedra*." He then retrieved the burro's reins from him. "You are a guest in this country, *pendejo*. An unwelcome guest. Never forget that. "

Then he spit on the ground, picked up his gear pack and put it on his back. He yanked on the harness attached to the burro and we resumed walking.

We spent the next half hour trudging on muddy ground in complete silence. I didn't mind. It was a break from my uncle's verbal abuse and at least I got to be with Pedro. Pedro was a real trooper. He just kept moving while he hummed some popular tunes under his breath.

We each had a backpack and the burro carried our extra necessities. I had brought my journal as well. From this point on I decided to make notes on the route we were taking to Tikal. Landmarks, rivers. Just in case Carlos decided to hit us with any more surprises.

But I had a surprise of my own. Remember that I mentioned that I had some extra protection? Well, I carried a pistol which I had smuggled into Guatemala. I kept it inside the waist of my pants. Guatemalan Immigration in Puerto San José wasn't very thorough. Still, I took an awful risk. So why did I bring it? Well, you never know, *amigos*. In the jungle anything could happen. *Banditos*. Wild animals. Anything.

We trekked north into the tropical lowlands. There was a certain magic to it, being surrounded by the wild sounds of the jungle forest and lush green plants in overwhelming profusion. I'd never seen anything like it growing up in the streets of Los Angeles. Here in the Guatemalan rainforest we rarely saw the sun for all of the trees – kapok, palms, mahogany. Sometimes we sank into mud. Always we had to be careful of quicksand and venomous palm pit vipers. Because Carlos went ahead of us as our guide, Pedro and I were charged with leading the burro. We took turns. Pedro was quiet, but with each step he seemed less sad. For me this journey was an exotic means to an end. For Pedro it was the yellow brick road.

What did it mean to Carlos, who kept 15 paces ahead of us as he slashed through vines and chanted under his breath – words and melodies that were too low to make sense of? I kept a special eye on Uncle Carlos's machete which he brandished with skill and a bit too much aggression. If he chose to, he could do great damage with such a weapon.

We ended that first day exhausted and sweaty. Carlos had us set up camp on an embankment close to a nearby river. We needed access to water but without being too close to the crocodiles. There was a small waterfall and Pedro and I laughed with the joy of seeing something truly beautiful. Carlos made sure the burro was well watered and tied him to a tree where grassy plants grew that he could graze on. With the burro taken care of, Pedro and drank our fill of the running water, took off our shoes and shirts and let it wash over our feet, chest and hair. Carlos drank some of the water but kept his jeans and long-sleeved shirt on. He mostly just stood on the bank and watched us.

Afterwards, we set up our tents and built a small fire. As twilight came, so did the biting mosquitoes and the diseases they carried. Fortunately, Carlos brought quinine. He mixed it with tequila and made Pedro and me drink a small dose in case of malaria. He refused it himself, saying he'd been bitten so many times he was immune.

We had some canned goods. We heated the beans and corn in a pot over the fire. Carlos made us collect as much dry wood as we could find (not so easy, *amigos*, with all that rain and humidity!) Carlos said we had to keep the fire going, not so much for the warmth as to keep the animals of the jungle at bay. We heard roaring and screeches and death wails, so Carlos obviously knew what he was talking about.

After the sun had set and the jungle was as black as pitch, Pedro and I sat together talking, even singing a few songs. We were slightly tipsy from the quinine cocktail. I asked for more of the tequila, but Carlos refused. He said we had to make it last. That strange man was always so damned serious. That first night I invited him to sit with Pedro and me but he refused. Carlos always sat apart. He didn't sing and he only talked when he had some instruction to give. That night and the subsequent two nights I would hear him chanting to himself. He always kept the machete within reach. A few times I caught him staring at me. Was it loathing? Was it jealousy?

I kept the pistol handy – especially after we went to bed. It wasn't just to keep away the jaguars. I worried about getting up to piss, having Carlos unexpectedly mistake me for a jaguar and swing his machete at me. I realize how paranoid that sounds, *amigos*, but you didn't see the expression in his eyes whenever he looked at me.

Carlos kept a tent to himself which he didn't use because he stayed up all night watching the fire. He said he would wake me when he needed me to take over the watch, but he never did. Pedro and I shared a tent. I tried to picture what we must have looked like through Carlos' jaded eyes. Imagine two reasonably vigorous young *hombres* sharing a sleeping bag in the middle of the jungle. Maybe he fantasized about fingers and tongues exploring muscle, hair, lips, who knows what else. It sounds sexy, no? Well, Carlos would have been wrong. At least that first night. Pedro and I were too damned exhausted to do anything but strip and fall asleep. But even if we had decided to "make passion" all night long, it was none of my strange uncle's business. We were no longer under his roof. If he didn't like what we did in the privacy of our little tent, to hell with him.

But now that I've brought up the subject of passion, let me share something. As hard and as dangerous as this journey was, the longer we kept moving northward, the more Pedro seemed to relax, to become more his old self. Sometimes we sang. Sometimes we walked in companionable silence. When Carlos wasn't watching we held hands. Despite the hardship, the frequent rains and the bugs, the fresh air and physical exercise felt good.

The second day started out without incident and most of the morning was much the same as the first day – Carlos leading with his machete, Pedro and I taking turns leading the burro, avoiding mud and snakes. But then as we continued to trek northward, something strange happened. I started to hear suspicious noises in the jungle – the snapping of branches, the rustling of ferns. I got the distinct impression that we were being followed. I said something to Carlos. He looked backwards to where I was pointing and just muttered to himself. I could hear slurs against me under his breath. I warned Pedro as well and he said that he didn't hear a thing – that I was probably just tired and hungry.

Carlos raised his machete high and sliced through a sapling that blocked our way. "Whatever you imagine you hear, *pendejo*, we do not stop until we reach the Rio Gordo. We continue." And he moved forward slashing at vines.

Quietly, I gave the burro's reins to Pedro and whispered to him to keep going. I would stay back just for a few minutes. Just to satisfy myself that I wasn't *loco*. "Don't worry," I said. "I'll be fine." Pedro looked at me with concern, but I grasped his arm to reassure him and he moved forward. I patted my waistband where I carried the secret pistol.

After only two minutes or so, I heard it again. The rustling. I hid behind a mahogany tree and watched to see who – or what – was following us. More rustling and I could see the brush sway with movement approaching the clearing I had just vacated. Then there was a final snapping of twigs and slapping away of leaves and I saw nothing. Impossible, no? But there was literally nothing there. That or else what was there was invisible. I spoke to it. I said "show yourself!" I heard nothing but the wind in the trees. Then, out of nowhere, I heard the roar of a jaguar! It was loud, and it was coming towards me! I pulled the gun out from my waistband but had nothing to aim at. There was nothing there! I stumbled backwards in terror and landed on my butt. I dropped the gun and lay there shaking as I felt fur brush against my arms and the feel and smell of a hot animal breathing in my face.

"Are you coming, *pendejo*, or not?" Carlos yelled out from a quarter mile ahead. For the first time in my life, I was glad that he was here.

The invisible jaguar rubbed its fur against me again and then left. I could see where the bushes and vines were pushed aside and I could hear the twigs and branches break as it ran off. I stared after the jaguar I could not see.

"Mundo, are you coming? It was Pedro's voice.

"Don't make me come back after you, *pendejo*." That was Carlos.

"I'm coming," I shouted, hoping they didn't hear the trembling in my voice. "I just slipped and fell on some wet leaves."

Still shaking, I picked up my pistol and put it back in my waistband. I decided not to tell what had happened to either Pedro or Carlos. I didn't want them to think I had gone *loco*.

But then I looked down at the mud where the phantom jaguar had been. There were prints there alright. The prints of bare human feet.

Hours more of slogging through the jungle. I hid my secret and pretended everything was normal. In fact, after two or three hours of hiking through the humid heat I began to think maybe I was imagining things. Something like a waking dream maybe. As we continued to move forward, I never again heard that rustling or the sound of twigs snapping after us. Maybe whatever phantom was haunting me had lost interest. But just when I had finally convinced myself that the entire thing had been a hallucination, I reached to scratch something on my upper arm. I felt something strange where the invisible jaguar had pressed against me. I touched the spot and lifted my finger up to examine it. It was some kind of blue paint. How in hell...? The next time we passed a creek I washed it off my arm. And still I said nothing.

At one point we stopped to drink and urinate. Carlos went off a ways, presumably for privacy. Pedro then came to me and smiled shyly. "I was worried about you back there. You seemed so strange. And you've been so quiet ever since. Are you better now, Mundo?"

"Sure, Pedro. I'm better."

"Good. Because I want to give you something."

"You do?"

And with that Pedro pulled my face to his and gave me a deep, long kiss. I could barely believe it. He'd been so cold to me for so long. Sure I kissed him back. He was the only person on the planet who could make me feel half-way happy.

We heard the rustling of Carlos returning and pulled apart, trying to act casual. Carlos just looked at us, asked if the burro was properly watered and then said for us to move on.

By the time we made camp that second night Pedro was as close to being his old self as I could remember. We ate our dried pork and canned beans. We each had a sip of tequila. Once we were finished with dinner, Carlos got up and said that he would be look-out. Pedro moved closer to me as we sat by the fire with Carlos about 20 feet away chanting something quietly to himself in the dark. Since we were sitting with our backs to him, Carlos couldn't see that Pedro's hand had landed and stayed on my crotch. I looked into Pedro's eyes questioningly and he nodded with a slight smile. We decided to turn in early. We said *buenas noches* to Carlos and he nodded to us without missing a word of whatever it was he was chanting to himself.

As soon as we were in the tent our lips locked together and we quietly pulled off each other's clothes. Neither of us had shaved for days but that was okay because the feel of our stubble rubbing together made the encounter even more exciting. That's when we made love for the first time since Magdalena and Roberto had died. Despite the admonition to be neither seen nor heard, we rolled around on each other – tasting, stroking, grasping, gasping – with Carlos not twenty feet away. We joined bodies to the music of jungle screeches and the occasional roaring of predators. I no longer cared if Carlos could hear us or not. Pedro's lips, his hardness, the scent of him, the fiery words he spoke inflamed me. Our bodies became one and our steadily mounting rhythm was as natural as the jungle. Pedro breathed hard in his attempt to control the animal sound of his pleasure, and my own climax was hissed through gritting teeth to try to avoid being heard. Why should I have cared? It had been so long since we made love! But whether our passion could be heard or not, the joyous laughter we shared afterwards could not be contained. *Ay, amigos,* you will never understand how much I loved him. My Pedro.

In the morning I awakened smiling to the sound of birds and monkeys chattering. Carlos was scouting our path and said he would be back in half an hour. Pedro and I went down by the river and, careful not to attract the crocodiles, bathed in the nude. We decided to shave and look like civilized men. By the time Carlos came back we were dressed and ready to go.

In addition to many other things, my strange uncle was a prude. He not only forbade displays of affection. He wanted to see as little skin as possible. His prudishness now collided with my need for comfort. The shirt I had just put on my back was now soaking with sweat.

You ever spend a lot of time in the rainforest? 95 degrees maybe with 95% humidity. Like nothing you've ever experienced. The sweat gets in your eyes and the idea of putting a shirt on your back seems crazy. It's true, as Carlos warned, that an unforgiving sun and the carnivorous mosquitos attack every inch of you if you don't. Then you walk around in a bath of your own blood and sweat. But on the morning of that third day – the morning after Pedro and I had made love – I decided to ignore Carlos' advice. "Screw it," I said. I pulled my dripping shirt off my back and tied it around my waist. I scratched at a bite that was on my neck. "The frigging mosquitos get you whether you're dressed or not."

What I did was nothing to me. This was the tropics – far hotter than a day at Santa Monica Beach in L.A. In prison, men removed their shirts all the time when working out. But my uncle reacted strangely to the sight of my bare torso. He stopped what he was doing. He told me to stand still. Then he walked around me inspecting my shirtless chest, my belly, the tattoos, my prison scars and some serious muscles from three years of working out. I couldn't quite get Carlos's expression. Was it lust? Or was it something more... appraising? I started to speak. "What the hell...?"

Carlos rubbed his chest, shook his head and shrugged. "Remember that whatever you do, whatever happens to you – these things are what you choose, *pendejo.*"

"What in the name of hell are you talking about, Carlos?"

He smiled that cynical smile of his. He touched my bare back with his hand as if checking to see if I had been properly cooked. He rubbed my sweat on his dirty pants, grabbed the burro's harness and said, "let's move on."

And so we did.

CHAPTER 6: TIKAL

That third day was mostly uneventful. Mahogany trees and toucans, snakes and butterflies all lose their wonder when you're sweaty and exhausted. The sounds of monkeys chattering and of unknown creatures squealing was beginning to get monotonous. At least this day I had no strange visitations from phantom jaguars. And this third night was very much a replay of the night before. Carlos sat alone staring at the fire and chanting to himself while Pedro and I ate, drank our tequila with quinine, talked, sang and eventually retired to our tent to rub flesh upon flesh.

I will say this. There was nothing monotonous about "making passion" with Pedro. Of all the men and women that I've been with – and up to that point, *amigos,* we were well into double digits – Pedro was by far the most passionate and tender lover I have ever known. The sexual connection that we had that third night was probably the best I've ever had. That it was memorable is a good thing. You see, *amigos,* that was the last time I have been with anyone. *Ay,* if only I could have understood what was to come.

Day Four was the day we woke up to the first of multiple disasters. Carlos's burro was gone! None of us had heard it, but someone must have snuck into our camp during the night, untied him and led him off along with the supplies he had been hauling. Who the hell would do that? Oddly, there were no footprints. It was as if the burro and our supplies had simply vanished. But I knew that there was nothing supernatural about this disappearance. It was *banditos*. Carlos had warned us about them during this entire trek.

But, dammit, he was supposed to keep watch! I got confrontational with my uncle. Where was he when the burro and supplies were taken? He said it was simple. He had fallen asleep. His eyes narrowed in anticipation of my accusations. "You are angry at me, *pendejo? You* are angry at *me?* I will remind you that it is my burro that has been taken." He started to fiddle with his machete. "I will also remind you that I'm the only one who has kept watch for our camp while you and *La Piedra...*"

I was about to shout back at him but something made me hold my tongue. "Never mind," I said. It was water under the bridge. But what were we to do? How were we going to carry the gold from Tikal without our burro? What's more, the duffel bags with all our clothes and other supplies were gone along with the canned food that was supposed to get us back to El Cruce. All we had now was the dried food in our backpacks, Carlos's machete and the clothes that we were wearing. Dammit!

Carlos looked surprisingly calm as he checked the contents of his backpack. "The government in Guatemala City tried to drive the jungle thieves out decades ago but could never succeed. Be glad, *pendejo*, that it wasn't the police who discovered us. Be especially glad that our throats were not cut during the night. Ah Puch and Buluc Chabtan were merciful."

Since I didn't believe in his "merciful" gods I changed the subject. "How will we get the gold back to El Cruce?" I asked.

"What we can carry on our backs will be enough. You will see."

Pedro chimed in. "And our lost clothes?"

He shrugged. "Clothing is cheap. We will make do."

I dressed with what I had and felt punished for the liberties I had taken the previous day. Sweat or no, I kept my shirt on.

We had a silent breakfast of pemmican, dried fruit and water from the nearby stream. We were hot and tired but, burro or no burro, we were only about five miles from Tikal. We walked as Carlos led the way with his machete. Then, as we slogged through the jungle, we heard thunder and it began to rain. Carlos did not react even though among the three of us we didn't even have a poncho to put on. Within minutes of the cloudburst Pedro and I were soaked and miserable.

Pedro had started the day in the best mood he'd been in for months. I already mentioned, we had made love again the night before. Memorable, passionate love. I was beginning to feel like there was real hope that we could make a future. In the weeks leading up to the trip, Pedro always had some sadness under the surface, you understand *amigos*? He could be silent or he could use cutting words the way he did that time on the *Doña Maria*. The last couple of days I thought he had snapped out of it at last. But now, with the burro getting stolen, the rain and the exhaustion, things started getting to him again – worse than ever. It was as if our night of love-making had never happened. He started muttering about how stupid he had been to come to Guatemala with me, how heartless I was to put him through this.

Heartless again! Dammit, if I was so damned heartless why did that kind of talk cut me like a knife? I didn't care if *Tío* Carlos heard and judged me. I told Pedro he was full of shit and reminded him that I had warned him about this trip. I reminded him of the gold we were going to collect. Did he want to go back to turning tricks with ugly. desperate men in the alleys of Hollywood? His jaw dropped with shock that I would say such a mean thing to him. Then he just spit into the rain.

We continued arguing like this as we trudged forward with Carlos completely silent when I unexpectedly walked right into a small stone wall-fragment. It was as tall as my waist, strangled by vines and had a jaguar image carved into it. This was the first physical outpost of Tikal. We were almost there! Pedro and I immediately stopped fighting as the magic of Tikal took over.

We encountered larger and more elaborate stone ruins until – awe-struck – we entered that massive complex of tall buildings and temples called *El Mundo Perdido* – the Lost World of Tikal. I forgot that my feelings were hurt and Pedro forgot that he was angry. I can still hear him murmuring "beautiful, just beautiful."

That *entrada* into Tikal is still like a dream to me. The archaeological site was enormous – I later learned that the main complex took up about one square mile of real estate. This was an amazing place of ancient stone temples and palaces engraved with hundreds of dream-images, all faded into time, eroded from the rain and wind and partially hidden behind a thousand vines and trees. I'd never seen anything like it in my life.

Carlos seemed to become more animated with the sight of each new structure. "There is the Temple of the Jaguar," he said. "And here is the Plaza of the Seven Temples." You could tell how proud he was of what his ancestors had built. My ancestors as well! Don't forget, *amigos*. I'm half Guatemalan, too. Uncle Carlos and I shared blood. I was heir to this stunning land through my mother, Catrina. Before this day I had never appreciated the magnificence of what my ancestors had built. Now I began to feel a pride I didn't know I had.

For all of you archaeologists out there, let me tell you a little bit of the history. Tikal was for many centuries the capital of one of the most powerful of the ancient Mayan kingdoms. Some of the monumental buildings there go back to the 4th Century B.C. Tikal reached its height during its Classical Period of 200 A.D. to 900 A.D. when it dominated much of the Maya region – present-day Guatemala, Honduras, Belize and Mexico's Yucatan Peninsula. Up to the year 900 A.D., think of Tikal as Central America's Rome. politically, economically, and militarily, as it interacted with areas throughout Mesoamerica such as the great metropolis of Teotihuacan in the distant Valley of Mexico. After that, some of the great palaces and other buildings were burned and by the end of the 10th century, Tikal was abandoned and forgotten. Long after it was lost to time, Tikal was rediscovered by archaeologists in the 19th Century. Of course, local people – especially those of Mayan descent like the ones who lived in El Cruce – never forgot about Tikal. That's probably how my mother and Uncle Carlos knew to head in that direction when they got lost as children. Now it was a much older Carlos who guided us into the main section of the ruins.

Just as we entered what had once been the Plaza of the Seven Temples, I tripped over a sharp rock buried in mud. I fell hard and the edge of the rock bit into my ankle. The pain was intense. I howled and fell backwards onto the ground. I could see that the ankle and shin were bleeding pretty badly in two places from where the rock cut into my skin.

Pedro immediately dropped his gear and helped me into a sitting position. "Oh Mundo, I'm sorry," he kept repeating. It was as if he was blaming himself for my accident.

Carlos came over to me without a word. He had Pedro move aside as he kneeled before me and removed the shoe from my bare ankle (all of my socks were lost somewhere in the rainforest with our stolen burro) and examined the injury. "It is not broken," he said. He poured water on the wounds but they continued to bleed. "*Joder*" he said under his breath. For those of you who don't speak Spanish, that's the "f" word.

He turned to Pedro. "Watch him," Then Carlos walked into the jungle and reemerged a minute later with a long dead branch. He handed it to me to use as a crutch.

"Do you have any bandages?" I asked. "The bleeding..."

"The wounds are not deep. With a tourniquet the bleeding will stop. We're almost there, *pendejo.*" He pointed to a set of steps leading up to the Pyramid of the Lost World. Then he took Pedro aside and they whispered together looking at me. After a few minutes Carlos again looked at my ankle. Then, to my surprise and despite our mutual loathing, he helped me stand and hobble over to the temple steps.

"Sit there and don't move. Here is more water. *La Piedra* will help you while you wait for me. I will find the *Templo de los Muertos.* And I will find something for your pain.

He walked off. Pedro and I sat on the ancient steps. I bent over to look at my painful ankle. It was swelling up bad and the bleeding wouldn't stop. With the theft of our burro and supplies, we had no spare clothing or cloth. There was no choice. Pedro washed my foot and ankle with some pooling rainwater. Then he had me remove and hand him my shirt which he proceeded to rip into strips to provide a combination bandage and support. My only shirt! How was I supposed to get through this expedition and back to El Cruce shirtless? With all the mosquitos and such, I'd get eaten alive! Plus, I had become self-conscious about what Carlos would say. How disrespectful I was to the gods, and so on. Well, what could I do?

I howled in pain as Pedro worked on the ankle. He didn't think it was a good idea, but I told him to place the shoe back on it. I still had to get around, no? When he was done Pedro pressed his hand against my chest and kissed me lightly on the cheek. "Mundo, how is it that you're always the one who gets hurt?"

"Just lucky I guess, Pedro," I said. He had me drink some water. Then we actually held hands while we waited for Carlos. With the tourniquet over my ankle the bleeding slowed considerably and the pain in my ankle started to subside to a dull throb. The rain stopped and we could see the sun shine bright through the clouds right into the Plaza. I caught my breath -- even in my pain it was pure magic. Pedro reached over to me. To my surprise, he put his hand on the inside of my thigh and kissed me on the lips. I was in far too much pain to be stimulated, but I placed my hand on his thigh as well. I was slightly surprised by his obvious sexual reaction to my touch. This was neither the time nor the place. but I think my vulnerability was getting him excited. I kissed his hand more with understanding than passion, and he again kissed me on the lips.

Just at that moment there was a loud crash of thunder. The mood turned ominous as clouds returned with astonishing speed, obscuring the sun. For a second I thought I heard drums beating, but I knew it was just my overactive imagination. Pedro and I huddled together as it darkened and the wind rose dramatically. A gust must have knocked a pebble from the top of the pyramid down the ancient stone steps because there was a long, drawn-out rattling of something all the way down the exterior of the pyramid.

Pedro suddenly gasped and jumped up. "What was that?"

"It was just a rock."

He looked at me with a frightened expression. "No, Mundo. Don't you hear that? That humming sound? And those voices?"

For a second I thought I heard drums again, but this was no time for hallucinations. "You're imagining things, Pedro."

He stood up and began to walk back and forth in front of me. "It's coming from everywhere! Make it stop!" Pedro was starting to act *loco*.

"There's nothing there!" I shouted. I struggled to stand and pulled him to me. "There's nothing there," I repeated, this time quietly. Then the pain got to me and I reclined back onto the step.

He abruptly let go of me and started pacing and moaning. "Why are we here? Why did we come?"

Before things fell apart, I decided to say something I had been rehearsing for the last month. "Come here, Pedro." He walked back to me and I took both of his hands in mine. "Because when this is over, we'll have enough money. I want us to start all over. I want you to be my life-partner, Pedro. Two men who live and love together. Maybe move to Florida. You said you've always wanted to see Miami. *¿Cuál es tu respuesta, mi amor?* What do you say?"

His eyes closed briefly as I tried to soothe him with my words. Finally, he opened his eyes, looked around and seemed to remember where we were. He took my hand and pressed it against his cheek. "Mundo," he murmured. "Do you know how long…?" Then he broke the connection and bent over to look at my injured ankle. "The bleeding has stopped," he announced.

"I don't care about the bleeding," I said roughly. "I care about you."

He was gentle but I could sense that he was not taking my offer seriously. "Mundo, Mundo" he said. He touched my arm and adjusted some of the hairs on my head. "I'm sorry about your shirt. How is the pain?"

Ignoring the question, I kissed him on the forehead and Pedro closed his eyes. I repeated my question. "I want us to share our lives together, Pedro. What do you say?" I pulled him to me. He put both of his hands on my bare chest. I think he was about to say yes. He opened his mouth but never had the chance to answer.

Uncle Carlos had returned. His eyes flashed rage. "Stop that!" he hissed. "I told you — neither sight nor sound!" He literally pulled Pedro off of me and then slapped my face. "Idiots! Both of you! You are no longer among mortals!" Pedro whimpered and Carlos softened his condemnation. "Look, if it's treasure that you want there is no time for your *maricón* love-making."

Dammit, Carlos! He had ruined our perfect moment and shamed my lover. I could have strangled him then and there, but... gold. I punched the stone stair and tried to stand but the pain was too intense. Pedro began to mutter to himself about offending the gods and the humming sound that was infecting his ears. Carlos ignored his unhinged behavior and presented me with some mushrooms he had harvested which he found growing near one of the ruins. "Take these," he said. "The mushrooms are ancient Mayan medicine. They will numb the pain." I sniffed at them. Were they poisonous or not? I didn't care. I scarfed them down. To my surprise, the pain receded to a dull throb within only a few minutes. They seemed to have a mild narcotic effect as well which gave everything that happened afterwards a slight dreamlike quality.

Dreamlike? Why am I beating around the bush with you, *amigos*? What happened afterwards was a nightmare, nothing less.

CHAPTER 7: PILGRIMS IN A LOST WORLD

As Pedro huddled on the ground hugging himself and I waited for the mushrooms' analgesic effect, Carlos described what he had found. He had located our target: the *Templo de los Muertos*, which was buried deep in vines and had been hard to identify. It was one of at least eight pyramids within the large complex of ruins. This was exciting news. This ordeal was almost over and I was closer to becoming rich than I ever had in my miserable life. I began to hear drums again. Then I considered that it might just be my pulse beating in my ears. I was getting a little bit loopy. The mushrooms were really starting to work. There was still pain, yes, but it was manageable. I stood using the tree-branch cane and nodded that I was capable of moving.

Carlos looked up towards a cloud-obscured sun that he could not possibly see. "It's noon," he said. "Now that you are capable, we must get going. We don't want to be forced to camp here tonight."

"Are you worried about the gods?" I asked perversely, recalling Catrina's snarky last words.

For once Carlos answered me with obvious sincerity. "Yes. I am worried about the gods."

Pedro stared at Carlos when he said this and then abruptly moaned. He stood up and put his hands to his ears. "The voices – they keep coming back! Help me, Carlos! I'm going crazy! Can't you hear them?"

He started to spin like a mad person. I grabbed at his hand and pulled him to me. "Stop this! There's nothing here."

"I hear them, Mundo, I hear them. The baby is crying!"

The baby? Sweet Jesus, I had to slap him to get him to stop acting crazy.

Carlos didn't react when I grabbed Pedro and slapped him but he must have seen how badly Pedro was trembling. He led Pedro to the bottom step of the ruin and had him sit. Then he had him consume a small mushroom with some water. Carlos grasped his arm between the elbow and shoulder and stared into his eyes as if he could will him into sanity. My strange uncle was actually capable of compassion and said words like *"Ay, ay La Piedra, esta bien"* along with some other words – Mayan, I believe – which I didn't understand. As Pedro began to calm down Carlos asked if he was alright. Pedro's eyes dilated and I could see the analgesic and narcotic effects calming him. Pedro then said that he was better but looked at me accusingly.

"You slapped me!"

I said I was sorry, it was because he was acting crazy.

"Don't you dare do that again," he snapped. He took a deep breath, shook the cobwebs out of his head and then, with a calmer voice, turned to Carlos. "What's happening to me, Uncle Carlos?" Carlos hesitated, then spoke with uncharacteristic gentleness. *"La Piedra,* the ghosts of Tikal – *las fantasmas* – do not speak to everyone. You are special, not crazy. Only those who belong here can hear them."

His answer calmed Pedro down but creeped me out. "'Belong here?' Now what the hell does that mean?" I growled.

Carlos pointed a finger at me and the harshness in his voice returned. "I was talking to *La Piedra.* Stay out of it, *pendejo.*"

Amigos, in that moment I realized how much I truly hated this callous young uncle. Then I remembered that he was Catrina's brother. No wonder he was such a jerk. He saw the murder in my eyes and it seemed to amuse him. "Come, my nephew. Let us get your reward."

I stood and tried to walk using the tree branch he had brought me as a cane but even with the Mayan mushrooms and the bandage made out of my shirt, I could still only hobble. Pedro had returned to something approaching normal and suggested I use the walking stick with my right hand and lean on him with my left. That worked. We were thus able to follow Carlos towards one of the ancient pyramids – neither the shortest nor the largest but the one with the largest roof comb – what looked like a small square house at the pyramid's peak. As we approached it, the bright sun reemerged and I heard a macaw screech at us.

In the last thousand feet before we got to the *Templo de los Muertos*, we passed a large flat-roofed building with a series of friezes on the side. They appeared to depict life in Tikal in ancient times. Farmers harvesting corn. Naked athletes hitting a ball with their chests. And a frieze which appeared to show a masked priest carving the heart out of a terrified victim. I shuddered. I had always thought that human sacrifice was an Aztec thing, not Mayan. I asked Carlos about it. His response was a hoarsely whispered *cállate*. Shut up.

We finally arrived at the foot of the *Templo de los Muertos* with its head peeking out of the surrounding jungle. Damn but it was so much taller than I was expecting! It was rectangular at the base and – according to the research I've done since this visit, 212 feet tall from the ground all the way up to the top of its roof-comb – that little square house at the top. I gazed upward and saw dark gray stone blocks piled one atop the other and shaped into a steep, twenty-story pyramid with at least a hundred steps going up. I'd never seen a structure like this, both beautiful and forbidding! But how in hell was I supposed to walk up all those stone steps?

"Not all of us climb upwards, *pendejo*," Carlos said, answering my unasked question. "Some of us go below."

"Now what in hell do you mean by that?"

He started to say something and then stopped himself. "Someday you will see," he said dismissively.

Between the pain I was in, the *in vino veritas* effect of the mushrooms and the fact that he was digging at me here of all places, I finally lost it.

"Stop dropping bombs on me like this, dammit! Today – right now – is 'someday,' Uncle Carlos. Not tomorrow and not next month. I want you to either shut up with your digs about the hell you think I deserve, brother of my whore mother, or stop hiding behind those glasses and explain once and for all what the hell it is that I did that makes you think you have the right to abuse me like this!"

He turned on me, removed his glasses for once and got in my face. He did not shout but spoke in a low voice, ominously. "It is you who have brought hell into it. It is you who has enraged Ah Puch and Buluc Chabtan. It is you who has torn the fabric of destiny. Just ask my murdered friend, Jose Garza!"

My eyes bugged out and my blood pressure climbed to a thousand over a thousand. His irrational invocation of those mythical gods! And why did he have to bring up Garza now? Would that fat married pawnshop owner who had been screwing my mother ever stop tormenting me? I exhaled. I stared into Carlos's eyes which visibly flashed with hate. I exhaled again and then murder entered my soul. Carlos had finally crossed a line where I no longer gave a damn about either gold or his ancient Mayan gods or the consequences of killing him. I just wanted my rotten, too-young uncle's poison blood.

I picked up my walking stick and with all the strength I had swung it at his head growling "You sonofa ..." I almost struck him but, fast as lightning, he ducked, pulled out his machete and brandished it at me.

Pedro screamed, "Carlos, no!" Pedro tried to pull the machete from his hands and Carlos knocked him to the ground as if he weighed nothing. That was the last straw.

I remembered my "extra protection." I reached for the gun that was hidden in my waistband. Panting, I pointed it straight at his chest. Again, Pedro screamed. But Carlos just looked at the gun and laughed with undisguised malice in his voice. "We're in the Lost World, *pendejo*. Guns won't work here. Nothing modern. Only knives. I dare you to try it. Shoot me." He stretched his arms out to either side looking for all the world like Jesus on the cross.

Pedro ran in front of Carlos to block me from shooting at him. Carlos laughed again, grabbed him by the waist, moved him and said there was nothing to fear. He taunted me again. "I dare you, *pendejo*, you lousy murdering bastard. You, who are the biggest mistake my sister ever made in her life! Shoot me. Shoot me now!"

Infuriated I aimed the gun at his chest, pulled the trigger and... nothing happened.

Stunned and even more furious, I again placed my fingers on the trigger. But as I tried this second time, he took his time placing his machete back into his belt, making sure it was just so. Then he walked calmly right up to me so that the muzzle of my gun pressed up against his chest. Then, seeing how I was shaking, he pried the gun out of my hand. "Only weapons of tradition work in Tikal," he said. "Knives. Swords. This machete. It is the will of the gods." He toyed with the gun briefly and then pressed the gun muzzle against my bare chest.

Pedro screamed. Carlos pulled the useless trigger, said "bang," laughed uproariously and then threw the gun far into the jungle. "Dead weight," he said.

I could have fainted right then and there but I fell onto my knees from being nearly shot by my own gun.

Carlos took a swig of water from his canteen. Then he looked to Pedro. "Tell your Mundo that we're wasting time." Pedro didn't react, frozen in horror from what had just occurred and distracted by the voices only he could hear.

Carlos came over to me, took my arm and lifted me up, his tone impossibly light after what had just occurred. "We are family, *pendejo*. What's a little squabble between an uncle and a nephew? Let's waste no more time. Do you want the gold or not?"

I was revolted by his touch but willed myself not to react. I closed my eyes wishing I were anywhere but here. When I opened them again Carlos was looking at me knowingly, expectantly. I heard the sound of birds cawing in the distance. Vultures no doubt. Just like my uncle.

Carlos gestured to us to follow him. I wanted to smash that handsome, too-young face of his into the rocks, but he had both outsmarted me and outweaponed me. I wanted to give up. I wanted to lay down in the mud and die. I hated Carlos and I hated Tikal and I hated everything about my life.

Carlos circled back to me. "You are so close, son of my sister. Why would you consider stopping now? Inside the pyramid is enough gold and jade to last you forever. Isn't that what you want?"

Pedro came to me also but with a different message. "Let this go, Mundo," he said. "Look at what it's doing to us. Let's get on a ship and go to some island in the Caribbean. We don't need the gold." He glared briefly at Carlos. "Not at this cost." He then put his hands to his ears and from where he stood began to scan everything with his eyes – as if searching for the source of his imaginary voices.

Carlos shrugged. Then he pulled something out of his pocket. It turned out to be two things in a small velvet pouch. One was a gold piece. The other was a lump of jade. He put both in my hand and told me to feel them, to hold them to my heart, to know that there was an entire room full of gold and jade treasure only meters away.

The jade didn't interest me, even though it was more precious to the Mayans than gold. No one makes coins out of jade. No one melts jade down into fungible ingots. No one gets married with a jade band on their finger. Marriage. I looked at Pedro whose eyes were still closed. I loved him but I knew somehow that the only way I could make it work with him was if we had money enough so that he would never again have to turn tricks and I would never again have to smuggle and steal.

Gold enough to live, I repeated to myself over and over. *Gold enough to live*. I made my decision and nodded curtly at Carlos. Pedro closed his eyes and moaned, but Carlos smiled. He put the gold and jade back into his pocket and gestured for us to follow him. I took Pedro's hand. "Come on, " I whispered to him. "Let's follow the bastard." Apparently, Carlos heard because he raised his hand high over his head and flipped me the bird without even bothering to turn around.

My ankle was swollen and painful but the Mayan mushrooms had made it possible for me to stand and walk. Fortunately, despite all those steps I had seen at the front of the Temple pyramid we didn't have to do any climbing. We remained at ground level. Carlos led us to the right of the Temple's grand, steep staircase to the side of the pyramid's base where a series of bas reliefs were carved. I groaned and again heard the distant beat of imaginary drums. We reached a section of wall that looked like it had been cleared of jungle foliage. Embedded into that section of wall was the carving of a huge *calavera* – a skull.

"This *calavera* is the entrance into the Temple," Carlos explained.

As disturbing as the idea of passing through the open teeth of this skull into the Temple was, it was equally weird that the jungle unexpectedly ended in a twenty-foot radius away from this entrance. It's not like the area had been cleared away by human effort. No, *amigos*. Branches of trees, ferns, vines – all green things turned black or ashen once they reached that point. As if even the Guatemalan flora knew to stay the hell away.

I pointed this out to Carlos. I wondered if there had been a fire or someone had come and spread poison. Bah, he said. There was no poison. Anything that was strange here was due to the *malo* that existed inside – the evil.

He took off his sunglasses and looked right at me as he repeated the word "malo." It was as if he were accusing me of being responsible for whatever evil emanated from the stones of this horrible place.

At this point, I heard Pedro moan. He was clutching his stomach like a pregnant woman. His eyes were glazed over. He gasped and very clearly said the name "Roberto" which sent chills down my spine. *El niño*. My dead son. *Our* dead son. "Pedro!" I shouted. I shook him to get him to snap out of it. He repeated "Roberto" again and I slapped him. His eyes focused. It took him a moment to remember where we were, what we were doing. "I'm alright," he said, though his voice quivered.

Carlos took his machete and pressed it into a slat between the eyes of the *calavera*. As the sky again darkened and the sound of imaginary drums beat in the distance, the entrance of skull teeth slowly yawned open and revealed a dark corridor of roughly hewn stone. Thunder rumbled. I heard a jaguar roar. I looked down and saw bare footprints lead right into the solid rock.

"And now, *peregrinos*, we enter the pyramid," Carlos said in a low voice.

"Peregrinos" means pilgrims. Trust me, *amigos*. We were anything but.

CHAPTER 8: THE PYRAMID OF THE DEAD

I had dreamed of this moment for so long – to enter this temple of wealth! To know that once I passed through this portal my life would change forever! My heart was racing, and I took a deep breath. But then just as I was about to step into the darkness Pedro grabbed my arm and cried out, "Mundo, I can't... They're haunting me! Make them stop!" Again, his eyes began to glaze and he looked as if he didn't recognize me. I shouted "Pedro, for Chrissake..." He put his arms around me and held me tightly. "Oh, Mundo. Can't you hear them? Can't you hear Magdalena and Roberto calling to us?" He wiped a tear from his cheek.

My heart stopped for a second. I looked at Carlos. His expression was inscrutable. "The spirits have sought *La Piedra* out. They want him here," he said.

I yelled "shut up" at him. Then, even as I told Pedro he was imagining things I started to hear a very light noise in the distance -- the drums again. But this time they were joined by a hissing sound like the suspirations of thousands of insects in the distance. It was unnerving. "What's that humming?" I asked.

"You hear the voices?" Carlos looked at me with more respect than usual. "Maybe... just maybe you belong here, too, son of my sister. Perhaps you are the beloved of Ah Puch."

Ay, my uncle once again invoked his myths at the expense of my sanity. I wanted to strangle him. I wanted my ankle healed so I could pick Pedro up and carry him far away. I wanted to run away myself, but we were so close! Something pulled me forward. *Gold enough to live* I told myself and the noises in my head stopped.

"We're running out of time," Carlos said quietly.

I turned to Pedro. "Can you keep going?" I asked. Slowly he nodded his head.

"Alright, Carlos. Lead the way," I said.

Carlos then entered into the black corridor. As he passed the lintel, I heard some unfathomable words escape his lips as he briefly pressed both of his hands onto the sides of the entry. I imagined that I heard whispers emanate from the pyramid. I imagined the earth shaking but it was just me trembling on my injured ankle. With Pedro next to me helping me hobble forward, we entered into the *Templo de los Muertos*. Once all three of us were in the corridor we heard wind, as if the corridor were audibly exhaling air into the jungle, like some moaning whisper of the gods.

Pedro began to shiver. He backed away from me and said he couldn't go any further. But I couldn't leave him, and it was hard for me to walk without him. I held my hand out to him and promised to protect him no matter what.

"No matter what?" he whispered. I took his hand and pressed it to my heart.

He took my arm and we moved forward through the dark and musty corridors of the Temple of the Dead. Carlos was quiet but clearly excited. With his flashlight he pointed to where the walls changed from very rough hewn to smooth. He explained that this pyramid was actually a series of pyramids one built on top of another – almost like Russian dolls – going back many ages in time.

Where Carlos was proud, Pedro and I were terrified. *Amigos*, how do I describe this evil place? Darkness. Pure darkness. We had to rely on Carlos' flashlight since the ones Pedro and I had brought were stolen along with the burro. Fortunately, there were also some slits in the rock face which allowed some of the jungle-dappled sunlight to stream in.

We walked single file down a corridor rife with cobwebs and the sound of dripping water. It was too narrow, with a ceiling that was too low and carved with a hundred forms of glyphs. It was cold. It had been in the 90s outside. Here it was probably in the low 60s. At this point I was wearing nothing but my pants and shoes with the remains of my only shirt ripped into bandages for my injured ankle. The sweat on my bare back actually made me shiver. "D-damn whoever stole our b-burro with my c-clothes." I was shaking so hard I stuttered.

Carlos looked at me oddly. He had us stop at a section of the tunnel which divided in two directions. He asked about my ankle, which surprised me. Then he dug into his backpack. To my surprise he removed some kind of Mayan cloth embroidered with birds and snakes and handed it to me. "Put this on before we enter the sanctuary."

"Is that what you've been guarding so closely, Carlos? Some old cloth?"

"You do not understand, *pendejo*. It is an offering to the gods. Do not think they are unaware of our presence. They watch us. They weigh our hearts. They will not allow us to take their treasure – their gold and jade – with neither ceremony nor gift. But for now, this cloth may serve two purposes. Put it on your shoulders." I took it and put it on as a shawl. My imagination was working overtime. I thought I heard the corridor sigh when I did so. But I immediately felt warmer.

Pedro said nervously, "Did you hear that?"

"It's just our imaginations, Pedro. The dark corridors, all this nonsense talk about the gods."

"You're a fool to disrespect Ah Puch and Buluc Chabtan in their own temple," Carlos said to me sharply as he displayed that jagged grin of his. "But whether you believe or not is unimportant. *Las fantasmas...* they like you being here, *pendejo.*" As he was about to pick up his backpack he hesitated, almost as if he were listening to something. Under his breath he said, "I understand." Then he turned to me, put his hands on the Mayan shawl and adjusted it around my neck almost like a lover. And when he was done, he didn't let go. "The spirits like you," he repeated. He ran his hand across my chest like a lover and then to my shock boldly grabbed one of my nipples and squeezed it into pain. "Just testing for them," he mocked.

I flung his arm away from me. "Don't play games with me, damn it! You're my uncle! Act like it! Touch me again and I'll punch you in the nose."

"Punch me in the nose, eh?" Carlos unexpectedly roared with a laugh that echoed maniacally through the stone corridors of this massive pyramid.

Pedro tried to quiet him. "Shhhh" he said. "*Cállate.*"

Carlos actually grinned. "Both of you are such children. There is no hiding that we are here, that we are trespassing in the presence of Buluc Chabtan and Ah Puch! If we are here it is because they allow it." Then my uncle spit on the hard floor and spoke in a normal tone of voice. '*Bueno. Vamanos.*"

The corridor narrowed. Now that we could only walk single-file I could no longer lean on Pedro for support. The walking stick helped as Carlos led the way through a maze of darkness. I could hear the echo of our footsteps reverberate throughout the temple. We finally reached a huge rectangular room. "This is the *Cuarto de Sombras*" he announced.

The Shadow Room.

I could not see this rectangular room well from the light of Carlos's flashlight. I could tell it was a vast chamber, but could only see what was a few feet ahead of me at the – what appeared to be the chamber's front wall before which stood an imposing stone table. In front of the table rested four large clay bowls, each one perhaps two feet in diameter. Carlos removed some matches from his pocket and ignited the contents. These bowls were Mayan ceremonial torch-pots and once they were lit, they illuminated the room with a ghastly, flickering fire.

As Pedro began to shiver and press his hands to his ears, I took his hand and whispered "Courage, *mi amor.*" Then I let go and began to inspect this remarkable room. I would guess its dimensions to be about one-hundred feet long by forty feet long. The ceiling seemed disproportionately low for such a large room – only about 10 feet high. The walls were full of elaborate carvings and paintings, many of which, though ancient, retained vivid red and green paint. The forty-foot-long east wall contained carvings which were bizarre as hell. The faces of gods, I would guess – skull-like and carved into a checkerboard pattern with every other square either raised or depressed into the wall. I never knew the Mayans created art of this nature. It was highly sophisticated and creepy as hell.

Carlos pointed up to the ceiling and explained that nine stories above us – just under the pyramid's prominent roof-comb – was the Great Ceremonial Hall. It was a vast shrine to Ah Puch and Buluc Chabtan which was a mirror image of this vast room. Apparently, the Mayan priests performed only some of their dark magic in the open before the people. Much of what they did was hidden in this *Cuarto de Sombras,* this Shadow Room. As I continued to try to understand what I was seeing in the flickering firelight, my attention was again drawn to the long, high rectangular table made of gray stone which delineated the front of the sanctuary. It was clearly an altar. On its side were bas relief carvings of what I took to be four priests.

"Is that what I think it is?" I asked.

Carlos confirmed its status. "*La Piedra Sangrante,*" he said. The Bleeding Stone.

I didn't like the sound of that. It meant one of two things. I deliberately ignored the sinister interpretation. "How does a stone bleed?" I joked.

"Don't ask stupid questions, *pendejo.*" was his terse response.

I steeled my jaw. He was right – it was a stupid comment. The mushrooms working on my ankle pain made me feel slightly drunk as I became transfixed by this slab of rock. I pictured it stained red with the blood of countless human sacrifices. I shuddered. The cold was getting to me again. The spell was broken when I heard Pedro begin to whisper to himself again. "Stop it, Pedro!" I said. "This is creepy enough." He left my side and went over to the wall where all the raised and depressed squares were. He took his backpack off and sank onto the floor, sitting with his knees pressed against his chest and staring into empty space.

I tried to pull him back to standing again but Carlos said to let him rest. We were almost there.

As Carlos and I approached the Bleeding Stone the humming and drumming sounds grew louder in my ears. I heard Pedro whisper "It'll be alright, *mijo*. It'll be alright." I hugged the Mayan shawl to me. It's not just that I was cold. I was trembling with the knowledge that Pedro was talking to what he thought was the ghost of our little Roberto, the *niño* who would have made us a family. This place was so creepy, and the narcotic effect of the mushrooms had left me so loopy that I began to think such things were possible.

When we approached the altar by the firelight of the torch-pots Carlos had lit, I noticed two more clay torch-pots just behind it. Carlos went to them and lit them. Even if it gave the distinct impression of Halloween, the more light the better.

As we walked past the altar Carlos gestured for quiet. There, to the right of the Bleeding Stone, was a frieze of a single skull surrounded by various symbols in that pattern of raised and depressed squares. On one such square a stylized man appeared to be brandishing a spear. And on another square was a man brandishing a disembodied heart. Finally, we saw a highly stylized bird. "Quetzalcoatl" I said, identifying this god. Knowing little about the Maya I cannot know how the word came to my lips. But when I spoke the name, I saw Carlos nod at me with a canny smile. He then pointed out the still vividly colored frieze symbols which depicted the gods of this temple, Ah Puch and Buluc Chabtan. This was the first time I had ever seen depictions of these gods whose names he had mentioned. Ah Puch was mostly skeleton with a part of his flesh decaying away. Buluc Chabtan was depicted with a thick black line leading from his eyes down one of his cheeks and a knife that was stabbing something – or someone. As I recoiled from these figures Carlos chuckled. "I thought you had no fear of these gods, *pendejo?* Do you begin to respect them at last?" I heard Pedro moan where he was sitting and I... I actually slapped myself to snap out of the evil mood this temple tried to ensnare me with. "Let's get the gold and get the hell out of here," I said.

Carlos nodded. "Of course." He moved forward to the frieze of the *calavera* and then stopped so abruptly I bumped into him. Carlos ignored me. He muttered some Mayan words and placed the palm of his hand against the teeth of the *calavera*. Nothing happened. He tried a second time with different words. Again, nothing happened. Pedro, still sitting on the floor thirty feet away, began to laugh like a crazy person. I looked at him with horror and Carlos looked at him with pity as Pedro again returned to whispering to himself and rocking back and forth, looking like a specter in the firelight.

"The *fantasmas* who inhabit the bowels of this pyramid have begun to take his mind. We must not overstay our welcome," Carlos said. Then he took the machete from his belt and faced me. "Give me your hand."

My eyes grew wide. "The hell I will! What do you think you're doing?"

Without replying he placed the machete on top of the Bleeding Stone. He approached me showing me that both hands were empty. Intimately close, he reached for and removed the Mayan shawl, now stained with my sweat, from off my shoulder. He placed it against the *calavera* teeth as if expecting it to work as a key. Nothing happened except that I began to shiver again from the cold against my bare skin.

"Give the cloth back to me," I said.

He folded it and placed it onto the Bleeding Stone. "No, *pendejo*. I brought it as an offering to the gods. Now they know it is here. It must stay on the altar even if the sweat of your skin is not acceptable. You must give me your hand."

"Why?"

He startled me by using my proper name. "The dark gods require blood, Edmundo Lopez. If you seek to enter the realm of Ah Puch and Buluc Chabtan, your blood is the price of entry."

I turned to Pedro. Carlos's use of my real name seemed to startle him into paying attention. He got up from where he was sitting and took my arm. "No, Mundo. Don't do this."

"My ankle wrap – where I bled into the – "

"Fresh blood which carries still the echo of your heart. That is the price," my too-young uncle said.

"How do you know this?"

"I am Mayan," he said simply. "From the ancient bloodlines. The same as you through *mi hermana*. Look about you. Look at the faces of the men on these carvings. Do you not see yourself in their features? Why do you ask stupid questions when you already know the answers?"

I inhaled deeply and made my decision. "Remember, Carlos Lopez, that I am the son of your sister. Be gentle." I said. The humming sounds that I had heard as if in the far distance now grew louder.

Carlos took hold of my arm with a grip much stronger than I would have expected of him.

"I do what is required, nothing more, nothing less. The mushrooms digesting in your belly will help you cope." Then, with expert swiftness he took the machete from the altar and with the careful skill of a surgeon opened the skin of my left palm. I gasped from the pain and Pedro shouted "Mundo!" My hand was now wet with my blood but before I was even fully aware of this new source of pain, Carlos took my bleeding hand and placed the palm on the stone wall. When he did so, the pain immediately stopped. It was as if this wall had swallowed the pain right out of me! I stopped shivering as well. I was still cold but not nearly so much as before.

Carlos pulled my bloody hand back from the wall. The stain of blood was there but the bleeding of my hand had already stopped, and a scar had begun to develop. How was this even possible? Pedro took my hand, kissed it and held it against his cheek crying softly as I looked at Carlos in astonishment. He simply said "shhhh" and pointed to where the wall was vibrating.

I heard ghostly whisperings as the four-foot-high entrance slowly creaked open. And there, on the other side of the wall, was – darkness. But when Carlos shined his flashlight into that chamber, I saw a blinding array of gold and green. Inside this secret chamber was a king's ransom of gold and jade! I nearly stopped breathing from the magnificence of all this wealth.

"The Treasury of Tikal," Carlos announced. "What are you waiting for, son of my sister? Enter the vault of the gods. This is what you have wanted, is it not?"

CHAPTER 9: THE PIT OF BONES

I bent down and stared into the Treasury paralyzed with awe. I was fascinated by the jade – I knew that it was the most precious of materials to the Mayans. But jade cannot be melted down and the objects made of jade were objects of art which I could not easily smuggle or sell. But the gold! We could take a fortune in gold, and it would barely make a dent in the wealth this room contained. Pedro stood next to me to look into the Treasury. With my now-scarred hand I took his arm and started to pull him in with me but he adamantly refused to cross that threshold. He was shaking. He looked at me and said, "No, Mundo, no! Roberto doesn't want us to." He turned from me and looked into empty space. "It's alright, Roberto." He was speaking to our invisible lost child as if Pedro were losing his mind.

Carlos ignored him. He handed me my backpack – the only thing I had left since the theft of our burro. "Take only what you know you can carry. The more you take, the higher the price."

What he meant by that was over my head. But with the way Pedro was worsening I didn't want to waste any time. Get the gold and get out. Find a doctor for my wounded ankle and get Pedro as far away from these Mayan *fantasmas* as possible.

"Pedro," I said, pointing him over towards the wall where he had been sitting before. "You sit here – don't move. Carlos and I will only be a few minutes." Pedro whimpered, closed his eyes, and moved towards the dark.

"Here," Carlos said as he lifted a large stick from behind the Bleeding Stone, thrust it into the flickering flames of the torch-pots and created a torch for me to see with.

I took it without speaking. I then bowed to be able to pass through the low entrance into the Treasury of the Mayan gods of war and death – the entire chamber glittered gold and green in the light of my torch and Carlos's flashlight. The beauty of what we saw took my breath away. The jade objects were exquisite – skulls, statuettes, masks. And there was far more jade than gold in this chamber. But there was plenty of gold for my satisfaction.

Most of the gold was beautifully carved or cast, but what mattered to me was that it was solid, meltable and fungible. What I was planning to take was not intended for the shelves of a museum, you understand *amigos*? I needed to transform metal easily into hard, green cash. And yet I could not keep from being dazzled by what I saw! By what my ancestors had crafted! I saw gods made of gold, gold vases and cups, gold implements intended for religious ceremonies. There were gold coins and cubes much like ingots. I saw knives of gold and I saw a pile of strange lumps that looked almost like coal – hundreds of them. The humming that I had been hearing in my ears grew suddenly louder as I picked one up. Looking at it curiously I heard drums begin to beat. Then I recoiled and threw it down onto the ground. It was shaped like a heart. A human heart made of gold!

Carlos had been watching me as I took everything in. He hunched over and carefully picked up the gold heart I had thrown down. I was startled to see him brush it clean with his shirt and then begin whispering to himself. He reverently lifted that gold heart up to the ceiling and then placed it in his pocket. The thought that my *tío* was a "thief of hearts" briefly entered my mind. What Carlos respected and what he held in contempt I could never predict. If he wanted to collect gold hearts, that was his business. I had a mission to fulfill.

I started sorting through this collection of priceless Mayan artifacts knowing I could only carry so much. I found a thin disk and held it to my torch. Etched into it I saw the markings of a canoe and some men wearing what looked like feathered headdresses. Next to this disk I found some very tiny golden bells, thimble sized. I shook them to see if they still chimed and immediately heard whimpering from the *Cuarto de Sombras.* "I'll only be a minute, Pedro!" I shouted.

"Don't let them get me!" he shouted in return. My anxiety was mounting by the minute. Insanity was getting to Pedro. I hurried as best I could. With no burro, the heavy pieces would be impossible for us to carry all the way back to El Cruce. So, I concentrated on the small stuff, always careful to separate the gold from the jade. I took the thimble bells, some objects that looked like coins, several small carvings or two. But not those gold hearts. I opened my backpack and filled it with what I thought I could carry on an injured leg. First, I counted gold enough for an expensive necklace. Then enough gold to buy a fancy car. Then a big house. Then, finally, enough gold to buy a juicy parcel of real estate on some commercial street-corner in Beverly Hills. This bag contained my future! Despite all of the weirdness of the site and my worries about Pedro I couldn't help grinning. Thanks to the wealth and greed of Ah Puch and Buluc Chabtan my life was about to change forever!

When I looked up from my binge of hoarding, Carlos hadn't moved and was simply watching me. He had taken nothing except for that one gold heart. Laughing, I said "Look at the gold and jade! What's the matter with you? Don't you want to buy a house?" He looked at me seriously and said "What for? There's nothing on this Earth that I require except for one thing. And no amount of gold will buy that."

"What's that one thing, Carlos?" I asked absently as I contemplated whether I wanted one or two bracelets.

"None of your goddamned business, *pendejo*."

I looked over at him, rolled my eyes and then resumed cherry-picking some of the small statuettes. "If you don't want the gold, why are you here?"

"You need to ask that, you stupid man?"

Something sinister in his voice made me stop what I was doing. I turned to him, the smile wiped clean from my face. My tone was serious and low. "Uncle Carlos, why in hell are you here?"

He hesitated as he picked up a statue of Quetzalcoatl and cradled it in his arms as if it were a baby. "I am here for the gods. And to honor the request of my sister, Catrina. I cannot explain more to you. You must learn to understand for yourself." He tenderly stroked the statue and then placed it carefully back in the pile of artifacts. "Let us not lose track of time," he said.

I didn't respond. I tried lifting my backpack and it was very heavy. My arms ached from trying to carry my filled bag. How was I going to get this back to El Cruce without the burro?

"Are you done?" he asked.

"Yes," I said. Carlos then led me out of the Treasury chamber. Carlos was about to seal the door when I yelled out *wait!* I had just heaved my heavy backpack over to where Pedro was waiting for us and – holy shit – he was gone!

"Pedro's gone!" I screamed at Carlos. "Where did he go?" As I tried to see Pedro in that massive room, the waving of my torch created fiery serpents in the air.

For the first time Carlos sounded weary rather than angry or sarcastic. He looked down at the temple floor as if ashamed. He removed his glasses and when he looked up there was a heaviness in his eyes. "There's only one place *La Piedra* could have gone," he said. He pointed down one of the corridors and then replaced his glasses.

At this point the humming noise which had retreated into the background loudly returned. Despite being shirtless, I began to sweat and felt my heart beating wildly in my chest!

"Carlos, we have to find him!" I shouted into the blackness of the corridor, "Pedro!"

I started to race towards the exit from the *Cuarto de Sombras* when Carlos grabbed my arm, making me drop the torch. He grabbed both of my shoulders and held me with surprising strength. "A hole has been punched into the world of the spirits. Edmundo Lopez. *La Piedra* has been summoned to fill that gap."

I yanked myself away from Carlos and picked up the torch. It was still burning. "We're wasting time! What gap? What the hell are you talking about?"

"Jose Garza. The man you killed."

I finally lost it once and for all. "Fuck you," I shouted as I started to chase after Pedro.

He again grabbed my arm to keep me from leaving and this time the strength he displayed exceeded all reason. "Listen to me, Edmundo Lopez. Listen for once in your pathetic life. I'm telling you the truth. There is a deficit, a reckoning that never took place because you interfered."

"You're out of your goddamned mind!" I shouted. I'm going to find him. And you're going to help me."

At this point he released his grip on me. "I will not help you. Do what you must. I will wait here and guard the sacred gold. You will discover for yourself."

I didn't even waste time on a glare. I grabbed the torch and headed out of the Shadow Chamber into a pitch-black corridor. Then Carlos said "Wait." Something in his voice compelled me to listen. He took a coil of rope from his backpack and handed it to me. "You will need this."

I looked at him numbly for a moment. I put the rope around my shoulders and then bolted into the corridor shouting "Pedro! I'm coming to help you!" There was no answer. Finally, I heard Pedro's voice – he was sobbing some ways behind me – down a corridor that I had already passed. His voice was echoing throughout the *Templo de Los Muertos*. I heard him crying. I heard him moaning "leave me alone, all of you! Just leave me..."

I got lost down a wrong corridor, retraced my steps cursing my injured ankle and the maze of corridors within this damned pyramid. It was like some diabolic hall of fun-house mirrors only instead of reflections, I was surrounded by Pedro's echoing, reverberating sobs. "Pedro, call out to me so I can find you!" I shouted over and over again.

He was sobbing, saying he couldn't stand it. Then, as the sound of ghostly humming in my ears grew louder, I heard him scream and say "¡*Vete!* Get back!" Then I heard another scream – a scream of mortal terror which curdled my blood! Then I heard a loud thud and Pedro's sobbing stopped abruptly. I felt my temples throb and my eyes pulse. I shouted "No, leave him alone!" I shouted without fear to whatever gods or ghosts haunted this horrible place. I both cursed and I prayed. But the silence was absolute.

Mi amigos, there are no words for the agony I felt in the pit of my stomach when I heard that sudden silence because I *knew*.

"Pedro!" I shouted hoping against hope for a reply. I called out to my uncle, "Carlos, help me!" But of course he never came. I retraced my steps in the dark, all the while shouting at the humming *fantasmas* to shut the fuck up. I remembered Sunday school and prayed to Jesus that Pedro would be alright. I again heard the humming accompanied by distant drums. It finally occurred to me to follow these phantom sounds. I hobbled slowly, carefully towards a hallway which was bathed by a strange jade-colored glow. I walked down that hallway following the voices until, at last, I came to an open ledge which overhung a pit. What the hell? The glow was there but too faint for me to identify anything.

I directed the light of the torch down into that pit so that I could finally make out what I was seeing. I had to try with all my might not to projectile vomit. There about twelve feet below me in a vast pit were the bones of dozens – no, hundreds of skeletons. These were not animal skeletons. I could see *calavera* after *calavera*, just like the carvings of human skulls etched into the temple walls. And there in this pile of bones was Pedro lying face down on the ground, utterly unresponsive to my shouts, my begging, my tears. "*Dios mio,*" I said to myself. "Don't let him be dead. Let him live!" The humming noise overwhelmed me. Once again, I shouted "Shut the fuck up!" This time, to my shock, the voices obeyed. This macabre chamber of horrors was plunged into silence. Now that the voices had stopped, I again called to Pedro over and over. He didn't answer but I thought I saw his chest expand slightly. He was alive! I knew that he was alive! I again called to Carlos for help, but it was useless – he would not come.

And yet he had had the foresight to tell me I would need the rope which was still hanging across my shoulder. How could he possibly have known?

I found a stone column, tested it for stability and then tied the rope around it. The rush of adrenaline I was experiencing nullified the mushrooms' soporific effects. As a result, the pain in my ankle had returned big time. Well, injured ankle or not I powered through. First, I dropped the torch onto the floor. Then I rappelled into the pit, my anxiety at fever pitch.

Once I reached the bottom, I retrieved the torch, stepped over the bones of the dead and hobbled over to Pedro lying on top of somebody's broken rib cage. I kicked the bones out of the way and shook him. Pedro didn't respond. I felt for a pulse. He was alive but barely. I put my mouth to his to begin mouth-to-mouth and I tasted the exhalation of his breath. Alive, yes, but obviously close to death. There was a big gash on his head, and he was bleeding. What insanity could have caused him to fall into this pit of horrors?! Did the tormenting ghost voices beckon him to jump?

I aimed the torchlight past the bones to the walls of the pit to see if there was another way out. No. There was only one way out and that was up by way of the rope. And as I let the flickering light from my torch scan across this field of bones I noticed – sweet Jesus! – one of the skeletons had its rib cage cracked open. Not just one. Two, six, all of them! The rib cages of all of these poor souls had been cracked open. I fought a wave of nausea as I imagined scenes of great terror, heard the screams and pondered what malevolent force could have demanded the sacrifice of a human heart. Were they truly the names Carlos kept mentioning, Ah Puch and Buluc Chabtan? Could they be real? And were these dead skeletons who inhabited this pit the source of the humming I was hearing? I had no time to think of such things. I had to get Pedro up and out. To hell with the gold. I had to get him to a doctor!

At that moment I thanked God for my years in prison. I was strong, *amigos*. Physically strong. I had lifted weights the entire time I was locked up. Pedro weighed maybe 180 pounds. First, I climbed up the rope by myself carrying the torch and then positioning it on the ledge where it could still give us light. Then I rappelled back down and picked Pedro up. I cradled him in my arms for a moment as if I were carrying him to bed. I kissed his forehead. Then I got to work. Carrying both our weights up the rope would be a lot even for me, but I slung him over my shoulder and was just barely able to do it. I hoisted us both up the rope and back into the corridor. I again hollered out to Carlos for help knowing that doing so was futile.

I placed Pedro on the floor and put my ear to his chest. He was still breathing, but it was shallow and sporadic. At one point he gasped. I again tried giving him mouth-to-mouth – my thoughts were tortured as I placed my lips to his and tried to breathe life into him – but it didn't help. I'm no doctor, but when I was in prison, I spent a lot of time in the library and learned a bit about medicine. I was pretty sure that Pedro had a bleed inside his skull.

I lifted Pedro up as gently as I could and put him over my shoulder. I then retrieved the torch so I could see in the dark and limped all the way back to the *Cuarto de Sombras*. The humming voices had come back and, although they droned softly, they helped guide me back to the room where Carlos and the altar waited.

I kept talking to my lover even as I strained from the pain and weight, but nothing I said affected him. His breath was slowing. My Pedro was dying. When I finally reached the Chamber of Shadows, I saw that the fires in the torch bowls were still flickering before the altar. I stuck the torch in a socket on the wall. There was no place for me to put Pedro other than on the Bleeding Stone. A slight moan escaped Pedro's lips when I did so, and he began to shiver. I looked around wildly and saw the shawl I had worn earlier, the one that Carlos said was intended as a gift for the gods. I placed it over Pedro as a blanket.

At this point I was also shivering again from the cold. My exertions, the pain, my anxiety – I had rivulets of sweat streaming down my chest along with Pedro's blood. I collapsed panting onto the floor next to the altar in a hunched position as I tried unsuccessfully to stifle my tears.

CHAPTER 10: BEFORE THE ALTAR

As I huddled against the Bleeding Stone shivering and weeping, a figure emerged from a shadow in the corner.

"Carlos!" I exclaimed. Once I had entered the *Cuarto des Sombras* carrying Pedro, I had forgotten him completely. He had been there the whole time watching me. Just watching.

I went to him and grabbed at his arm. "We've got to get Pedro to a doctor! What in hell are you waiting for?!"

Carlos removed my hand from my arm with an iron grip and looked at me through narrow eyes. "We're a hundred kilometers from a doctor. We have not even a burro to help us."

Hearing this harsh reality caused whatever fragile hope I had left to evaporate. I collapsed onto my knees before the altar. My tears turned into big shuddering sobs. I was beyond caring whether or not my strange uncle witnessed my weakness.

I expected Carlos to laugh at me. Instead, he walked over and stood behind the altar. He picked up Pedro's wrist and felt his pulse. He manually opened both of Pedro's closed eyes and peered into his soul.

"*La Piedra* is not past the point of no return. Do you want to save him?" My uncle's voice was low, serious. I barely heard him. He returned to me as I sat crouched on the floor and slapped my face. Hard. He repeated his question: "Do you want to save your Pedro?"

"How can I save him?" I choked the words out between sobs. I had Pedro's blood on my arms and chest, I was shivering with the cold of that cursed pyramid and I finally realized that I was experiencing the rock bottom moment of my miserable, worthless life. "Pedro's dying and there's nothing I can do about it!"

Carlos then spoke words which echoed through the *Cuarto de Sombras* and pierced through my desperation. "There is one thing you can do, Edmundo Lopez."

The whispering noises that I heard returned and I looked at him with the hope of a child. "What? What can I possibly do, Carlos?"

"You can show respect for Ah Puch and Buluc Chabtan. You can repair the fabric of the spirits."

My eyes burned from trying to control my tears and I took Pedro's limp hand in mine. I was frustrated into despair. Carlos was once again invoking gods and spirits who I did not believe in and utterly rejected. "I don't understand what you're saying, Carlos." I turned away and stood up to again check Pedro's face.

Carlos inhaled so deeply I could hear it. "Do not turn your back on me. Please." This was the first time he ever said 'please' to me! Surprised, I turned again to face him. "I have tried to tell you. The man you killed - the man whose death you caused – Jose Garza. He was not important merely because he was your mother's lover. He was important because this man from El Cruce – my ancestral home - and yours – was a Mayan lord, a descendent of priests from this very temple."

At this point my weeping stopped and I began to feel a gnawing in the pit of my stomach. The whispering voices were suddenly silent as if Carlos had earned not only my undivided attention but theirs as well. I leaned back against the Bleeding Stone and faced him. "Go on."

"As a teenager, Jose was wild, devoted to the excitement and pleasures of being a handsome young teenager. We were best friends, he and I. And, I confess to you, sometimes more. But he was from better blood than our family. When Jose was twenty years old, he was formally dedicated to the god of war, Buluc Chabtan and the god of death, Ah Puch. To ensure the fortunes of his family and our people, Jose committed himself to the Sacrifice. But his ancestry as a Mayan noble made it possible for him to strike a bargain with the gods – a bargain of mercy which granted him time to live out the span of a normal life. And in the end – when the contract came due – he would give his living heart to them in exchange."

My fascination turned to revulsion. "What did you say? His living heart?"

He ignored my interruption. "Your criminal actions in Los Angeles caused Garza to die far away from this temple and without proper ceremony. By breaking that sacred agreement, a hole was rent in the fabric of the Mayan spirits. The life that belonged to Ah Puch and Buluc Chabtan, that Jose had agreed to pay to them, you stole." Carlos had grown increasingly strident as he spoke of what I stole. Then he glanced at Pedro, looked into my eyes and seemed to appreciate the torment I was in. "Perhaps it was not your intention, but you took that life just the same. They are angry, Edmundo Lopez. And when the Mayan gods of war and death are angry, they cause things like hurricanes." He looked at me pointedly. "Or cancer. Or death in childbirth. Or defects in the heart. Or insanity. We are none of us safe." Carlos spoke slowly as he recited a litany of the sufferings of those who had lived within my orbit.

I could barely breathe transfixed by what I had just learned. Cancer? Death in childbirth? Heart defects? What Carlos was saying wasn't possible, was it? The whispering voices suddenly returned with a crescendo and the drumming sounds, as well. I pushed my hands to my ears to try to drown out noise so loud it was painful. And in those loud, frantic whispers I thought I heard the voices of my mother, Catrina; my lover Magdalena; my baby son Roberto. And I looked down at Pedro's inert body. Would his voice soon join them? What had I done to them? I cried out, "No! It's impossible!" Carlos's eyes bored into me, and I could no longer stand. My back slid down against the Bleeding Stone and I ended up huddled on the floor staring at him like a wounded animal.

"In your heart, my nephew, you know that every word I tell you is the truth."

I covered my face with my hands and whimpered. But he had one more revelation for me. I somehow gained control of my breathing and spoke in a whisper. "Why aren't they after me? Why would they want Pedro instead of me?"

He looked me dead in the eye from behind the altar. "The gods recognized Pedro. For, you see, he is Jose Garza's son."

My head reeled for a moment as I remembered the weight of that dead man on top of me when he tumbled down the stairs during my aborted robbery attempt. "That's a lie!" I shouted.

"I do not lie to you, son of my sister," he said evenly. "Your one-time lover, Magdalena, was the daughter of a prostitute. *La Piedra* was Magdalena's brother, the son of that same prostitute and Jose Garza. Thirty years ago, Garza kept that woman for over five years. Pedro, the man you say that you love, is the son that Garza sired. When you killed Jose Garza – debtor to the gods and your mother's lover, you also unknowingly killed the father of both of your lovers. And the grandfather of your own son.

My jaw dropped as I continued to shiver with the cold and this bizarre disclosure. I whimpered. "How can you possibly know th-this?"

I stammered.

"Garza was my friend – when we were children, *sabes?* Well into our teenage years. And he was the man my sister hoped to marry even though he was of noble birth. Shortly after he made his contract with the gods, he left El Cruce lest complaining tongues wag. Plus, he wanted to see the world. That is when your mother followed him to *Los Estados Unidos*. Not just to pursue a hopeless love but to protect the debt of the gods. And that is when I became a brother in the blood."

"My mother...?

"She was faithful to the gods of Tikal. She was especially favored of the god of war, Buluc Chabtan." So that explained her unreasonably belligerent nature.

"And you are a priest of these gods?" I asked.

"No. I am not. Our family does not have the blood of lords or priests, son of my sister. I am merely an acolyte. But as my sister was favored of Buluc Chabtan, the god of war, so I am favored by Ah Puch, the god of death. With *mi hermana* dead, I now speak for them both. And time is running out." He bent over Pedro, looked at the wound on his head, checked his breathing and put his head to Pedro's chest to listen to his heart. Carlos raised his head up to the ceiling and appeared to be listening to something – or someone – that I could not hear.

"Time is running out," he repeated. "La *Piedra* may yet live, Edmundo Lopez. If you are willing." He was serious – dead serious and I knew it. I could no longer lie to myself.

"What do I need to do?" I asked. He didn't answer me although I saw his mouth curved imperceptibly into a grim smile. Carlos walked over to the checkerboard wall where the gods and *calaveras* were carved. He retrieved his backpack from the floor beneath them and brought it over to the Bleeding Stone. He then began to remove some types of

Mayan artifacts. Religious implements, I inferred. I then watched with a small thrill of horror as Carlos retrieved a mask from his backpack – an elaborate and terrifying mask of jade much like the ones I had just seen in the Treasury. I heard him chant some words in Mayan. Then he took sage from his bag and lit it on fire using one of the torch-pots. He blew out the burning sage which then became an incense which he blew onto the mask and onto the altar. He placed the smoldering sage onto a dish which was next to the torch-pots. The strange man who was my uncle then placed the jade mask over his face and returned to his place of power behind the Bleeding Stone.

The humming and drumming noises in my ears were becoming deafening. Uncertain of what I was supposed to do, I nervously stood up at the altar and again checked Pedro's condition. There was no improvement. I ran my fingers across his face and heard a slight moan, but he didn't react to my whispered pleas to wake up. His skin was cold and starting to become blue. Time was indeed running out. I gazed at that handsome face, that innocent face with a scar on it, that face with skin that was never perfect and a mouth that was a little too wide and I loved him more than I have ever loved anybody in my miserable life. As I took his limp hand in mine, I realized with the shock of complete certainty that if Pedro died then I no longer wished to live.

Pitiless eyes gazed at me through the slots of Carlos's jade mask. "Now you know the consequences of the death of Jose Garza at your hand. Now you recognize the ripples of consequence – how your careless actions have damaged everyone within your circle and beyond. Now you know of the wrath of Ah Puch and Buluc Chabtan, of the hole you have pierced in the fabric of the gods that must be filled – and why *La Piedra* was chosen in Jose Garza's stead. Now that you know all of these things, what would you do, Edmundo Lopez, son of my sister, to save this man?"

My breath was short and rapid. This was madness, wasn't it? Carlos was crazy. Or I was. But the humming noise dogged me. And the pain in my ankle again threatened to explode. I opened my mouth and then closed it. I didn't know what to say. And then I again looked down into my Pedro's face – a face that was not perfect but one that I had loved – as Othello put it – not wisely but too well. And I had killed his father. And now I faced the impossible question: along with the death of my mother, did my actions cause the dark gods of our ancestors to bring about the death of Pedro's sister Magdalena and his nephew – my son – Roberto in retribution?

Overwhelmed by the amount of damage I had caused in my life, I looked at the images of the gods of war and death carved in stone. So, Ah Puch and Buluc Chabtan existed after all. I swallowed hard, then decided that they did not scare me. I made my decision. I heard the whisperings and chanting of the *fantasmas* reach a frenzied crescendo as I raised my face towards Carlos. I stood as tall as I could and answered in a clear, sober voice, "Anything, Carlos. I would do anything to bring Pedro back."

CHAPTER 11: AH PUCH AND BULUC CHABTAN

Carlos sighed and nodded gravely. The ghosts also sighed, their whispers and drumming sounds melted into the background overshadowed by the loudness of the beating of my heart.

"We will save him then, this Innocent who deserves life." His voice was unexpectedly gentle. Carlos removed the Mayan shawl from Pedro's inert torso and adjusted his limbs.

I almost smiled even as I fought tears of anxiety. My Pedro, with his street-hustling past, his exceptional knowledge of male sexual gratification, being called an Innocent! But at this point Pedro was all that kept me alive. I looked at my backpack filled with Mayan gold and closed my eyes with shame. I had thought that the gold would give me a new lease on life, but I knew now that if there was no Pedro, I didn't give a damn about the gold. Whatever Carlos said Ah Puch and Buluc Chabtan required of me I would do.

"Are you going to kill me?" I asked dully. I was dead serious. I no longer cared.

"No, *hijo de mi hermana.* It is not your death that will repair the ripped fabric. You are going to make a sacrifice. But you will not die." He paused. "Not for a very long time."

"What do you want me to do?"

Carlos looked up at the ceiling as if he could see the sky through the frightening images of faded red and ochre paint covering the stone ceiling. Then he unexpectedly began to sing in Mayan. Without missing a beat, he dug into his backpack and removed an ordinary canteen. I stood perfectly still until Pedro gasped again. Carlos gestured for me to not move. He stood over Pedro and made a waving motion with the canteen in a zig-zag-like pattern, almost like the priests do before communion. In hindsight I believe he was invoking the spirits from the four directions. He then flicked some of the liquid directly onto Pedro's chest, then onto his head where the cranial injury was. I could see that the liquid was a luminescent milky pearl color. Carlos finally opened Pedro's mouth with his fingers and poured some of the contents of the thermos down his throat. Carlos followed this by inhaling some of the sage incense, then placing his lips onto Pedro's mouth and exhaling into him. This was a kiss which made my stomach churn but which I could not resent because Pedro instantly stopped gasping and, within a few seconds, I could see his breathing start to steady. Seeing was believing. My strange, too-young tío Carlos had access to powers I could not deny.

Carlos then turned his gaze to me and with a forceful gesture commanded me to kneel at the altar before the gods. What choice did I have when this man held in his hands the powers of life and death? I suddenly felt all of the cold in the room chill me to the bone. But as I slowly knelt, I also felt all the defiance I had ever felt in my life evaporate. Pain, the mushrooms, the adrenaline rush from collecting the gold, the imminent death of Pedro, the whispering of the Mayan ghosts, the accusing images of Ah Puch and Buluc Chabtan had removed all of the fight from me.

Carlos walked around the altar to where I was kneeling. The eyes gazing at me were like amber flames piercing through the jade mask. "Now you drink this," he said.

"What is it?" I asked softly, trying to keep my teeth from chattering.

"An elixir" he answered in a low, not unkind voice. "*Vida dentro de la muerte*. It is life within death. Even as we speak, it is saving the life of the man you love, *La Piedra*." He then put his hand on my shoulder. "And it will allow you to survive the sacrifice."

"Carlos, what is this s-sacrifice?" I was shivering worse than ever from the cold.

"Drink, Edmundo Lopez. All of it. Just drink."

I swallowed the entire milky contents of the canteen. At first, I was struck by how disgusting the flavor was. But after a few moments I felt like I had taken a swig of tequila. I began to feel warm all over and the temperature inside the temple not only felt tolerable but balmy. I began to feel more relaxed than I had in months. Everything was slightly blurry but appeared brighter. My heart stopped racing and suddenly as I sat up and looked around the *Cuarto de Sombras* I could see spectral shapes hovering against the checkerboard wall – an audience of spirits. The drums that I heard were now in perfect sync with my beating heart. The whispering sounds I had heard now became more defined – they were clearly voices. Suffering human voices. And as they began to chant, I realized that I had lost the ability to fight, to say no. Even time itself felt strange. In some moments it felt dilated. In others, it felt like it was speeding up. Edmundo Lopez no longer had a will of his own. At this point I belonged to Carlos.

"What do we do now?" There was no longer a shiver in my voice, but I asked the question from the bottom of a 100 foot- deep well.

Carlos put both of his arms under mine and heaved me up from my kneeling position. How strong he seemed in my weakness. "You must sit upon the Bleeding Stone." He guided me to the altar and helped me to sit up on it.

"Now, Edmundo Lopez, you will lie on the Stone, like so..." he placed his hands on my chest and laid me on my back. I was so warm from the elixir that the cold stone felt good on my bare back. To my surprise he rubbed some type of blue paint on my face and bare chest. Then to my shock he began to unzip my pants. "No," I growled.

He answered me in low tones. "This is their demand, not mine. If you wish to be accepted, I remove the rest of your clothing. You are being reborn and if you are to be theirs, no secrets shall be hidden from the gods."

My eyes bulged and I tried to sit up. "The hell you..." I couldn't even complete the sentence. I had no fight in me. I could resist nothing.

"This is as Ah Puch and Buluc Chabtan command it to be done." Then, with me as weak as a baby supine upon the altar, Carlos removed my shoes, trousers and underwear and threw them in a corner. I was naked, paralyzed and deeply ashamed to be seen thus by this strange young uncle.

I was barely able to get the word out. "Whyyyy?"

"I was there when you were born, Edmundo Lopez. No, not in California, son of my sister. But here in Guatemala. You are from El Cruce as much as I. As much as her. As much as Jose Garza. You are true Mayan down to your marrow. Just look at the shape of your eyes, the angle of your cheekbone, your forehead, every bit of your skin." He ran his finger across my chest, placed his hand on my belly but, thankfully, reached no lower. "You are *pura Guatemala*. That is your blessing. That is your curse." Then he unexpectedly grabbed my bare inner thigh and brought his face close to mine. "Do not be so arrogant as to think I covet the flesh of your body," he whispered roughly.

My eyes rolled questioningly to indicate Pedro. I couldn't bear the thought of his also being stripped and suffering this indignity.

Carlos understood and patted my arm reassuringly. "Do not worry for your lover. The gods do not require this of *La Piedra* – unlike you, he will not become theirs."

Become theirs! I was making a sacrifice involving God-knows-what to pay for Jose Garza and to protect Pedro! And now I was learning the truth about my own past. *True Guatemalan. I was born here!* This was too much to process. As I was about to die at the hands of my insane, degenerate uncle, it seemed only fitting that it be on the heels of another Catrina falsehood. Never once had she disclosed to me that I was born in El Cruce, that I was in truth Mayan – that she had sent me to plunder the treasures of my own people only to betray me to the gods. And where in hell was my father in all of this? Now I wondered again for the hundredth time who my *padre* was. He had to be from here. Garza himself? Some village boy? Surely not my strange *tío* Carlos – that would be unspeakable on so many levels. I tried to speak. I tried to move but each limb felt like it weighed 300 pounds.

Time slowed again. Then it speeded up. The light of fire and the pitch black of night both penetrated my brain. Naked or not, I could no longer feel my body. I could still hear the whispering background, but it gave me no sense of time. It could have been minutes; it could have been days. I have no idea how long it was until my next memories kicked in – those memories which haunt me to this day.

The sudden, unexpectedly loud beat of a drum brought me back to the present. I opened one eye and with it I watched Carlos complete rubbing that blue paint over my entire body, sparing not even *mis privadas.* I then watched as Carlos removed his own shirt and blue jeans. He was garbed now in only a traditional loincloth. He applied the same blue paint to his bare torso. With the otherworldly jade mask and his blue-tinged skin he looked like some type of evil spirit.

Now I began to hallucinate. I saw the *Cuarto de Sombras* fill with Mayan priests, some wearing only loincloths, some wearing toga-like robes, and all of their faces obscured by elaborate masks of either jade or gold. The whisperings that I had been hearing now blended into very specific chanting by this chorus of priests. I saw the scarlet and turquoise colors of the sacred quetzal bird fly over me again and again as Mayan acolyte Carlos danced and writhed and was joined by spectral priests and acolytes. I watched in horror as his eyes grew red. I then saw an extensive cross-like scar on his chest slowly become illuminated from within, highlighted by the blue paint upon his chest, until it looked like fire burning his body from within.

Carlos raised his arms and brandished some type of object made of metal and decorated with feathers. He called out, chanted and droned loudly in Mayan. I understood nothing of what he said until he began a litany of names which I have never before heard. But when I closed my eyes within my trance state, some part of my ancestral memories recognized the names: Kukulkán, the feathered serpent creator, Itzamná, the god of the sky and Ix Chel, the moon goddess. But it was when he recited the names I had come to dread: Buluc Chabtan, the god of war, and Ah Puch, the god of death that my body began to involuntary shudder. Deep in the marrow of my bones I realized that it was these two gods who Carlos served, evil gods who, in the darkest possible collaboration, desired not life but human sacrifice.

Then acolyte Carlos approached me as the ghost-priests chanted. I could no longer move my lips. My eyes said "no" but I could do nothing to struggle or protest. He placed a mask over Pedro's face. Just before he placed one over mine, I could see the materialized, enormously tall incarnations of Ah Puch and Buluc Chabtan take their place behind the altar. The last thing I could see before the jade mask blotted out my peripheral vision was that massive fire scar on Carlos's blue chest pressed right up against my torso.

Everything fell into blackness. And in the depth of that blackness the chanting and humming noises I heard took on shapes and forms. I felt them run over my naked flesh like insects. My body was blind and paralyzed but in my soul I screamed. I began to have visions. In my mind's eye I could see faint firelight and I saw Carlos hand an object to the incarnated Ah Puch. With a scowl he stood over me brandishing that object with feathers. Then I saw him put the feather object down and lift up what appeared to be a feathered object with a sharp blade. I inhaled sharply and suddenly felt as if I had been plunged into deep waters as I dissolved and somehow began to float. I was a massless spirit! You cannot possibly understand what I am saying, *amigos*. To this day I cannot understand it either, but I felt as if I had neither form nor substance. Surely, I was dead! I could now see with spirit eyes! I floated as if I were but a vapor. Below me as in a dream I watched Carlos shake that strange, feathered knife over Pedro and my inanimate body as Ah Puch and Buluc Chabtan, each at least 8 feet tall, stood next to him dwarfing him and staring down at me with fire eyes. I expected to see blood upon my chest but whatever that strange object was it did not pierce my flesh.

Now when I looked away from the Bleeding Stone, I could see other disembodied spirits. They called to me "Mundo, Mundo" as my spirit hovered over the altar. Jealous of my life force, I saw them float towards my still-living body and caress my face, my chest, my stomach, my genitals, down to the soles of my feet. Ghostly hands touched every inch of my material being while acolyte Carlos continued to drone and Ah Puch and Buluc Chabtan continued to stand motionless and commanding next to him.

Then I watched as a quartet of ghost-priests floated towards the altar. When they reached the Bleeding Stone each dipped a hand into one of the torch-pots and when they did so they became something in-between spirit and solid. They stood solidly on the ground, but they were still largely transparent. Carlos stepped aside and kneeled with his head down. The chief priest – masked, muscular and with a scowling grin – approached my naked, painted body as the others watched and chanted. He caressed my chest and then, to my surprise, plunged a ghostly hand *into* my chest. Then – and this vision nauseates me to this day – the chief-priest pulled what looked like the ghost of my heart from out of my chest! My spirit was floating as if I were dead, but I could see that my material body wasn't dead yet because that disembodied heart – *my* heart – was still beating. There was no blood as my chest had never been physically ripped open, but...

My disembodied self screamed again and again and again despite the fact that I had neither voice nor sensation! From overhead, I stared as that spectral heart solidified into fully physical tissue. It remained beating even though it was detached from my body. The ghost-priest lifted my disembodied heart and held it up for all the ghost priests and spirits to see. He shouted the names Buluc Chabtan and Ah Puch and all of the chanting ghosts repeated "Buluc Chabtan, Ah Puch" and then I saw the quetzal bird again fly through the *Cuarto de Sombras* and then disappear through the ceiling. The chief-priest then turned to Ah Puch and Buluc Chabtan and bowed low before them. He then ceremoniously removed the breastplate that Ah Puch wore and handed it to acolyte Carlos.

Ah Puch, expressionless, pitiless, came forward and now stood before the altar bare-chested. The chief priest shouted some words that I didn't understand even in my spirit state. Then I watched as my disembodied human heart began to grow invisible and immaterial again and, as it did, the ghost-priest raised it up and placed it against the chest of Ah Puch where it melted into him. Ah Puch then turned to Buluc Chabtan. As the chanting of the spirits grew into a feverish intensity, the god of war and the god of death grasped arms and touched lips. The sanctuary was filled with a blinding light as the two gods merged into one terrifying entity with four arms, four legs and two heads – a terrifying monster which stared out at the gathering of spirits with its four fire eyes.

The chief priest, his associate priests and the acolyte Carlos ululated as the unified body of Ah Puch and Buluc Chabtan turned and crawled on its four legs up the wall, onto the ceiling and then through the rock, presumably to the top of the pyramid. I never saw them again. The spirit priests chanted more and more slowly. The drumming sounds stopped and the crescendo of spirit wailing settled back into a whisper.

Acolyte Carlos now moved forward to the Chief Priest. He was holding something. I saw that it was the lump of gold that he had re-moved from the Treasury – the one shaped like a human heart that I had tossed onto the floor because it had revolted me. I watched as Carlos handed it to the chief priest who spoke some Mayan words over it. He then placed it onto my bare chest. That gold heart began to glow. Then it slowly sank down into my body as if my flesh had been made of a thick liquid, finally disappearing into my chest.

I again screamed silently with my disembodied voice. I saw the glow of the golden heart illuminate the skin of my chest throwing off striped shadows where my ribs were. Then I blacked out. I remember nothing else of that terrifying ritual.

CHAPTER 12: A HEART OF GOLD

At some point I was brought back into my body. I woke up with a shudder. My eyes were closed but I could hear Carlos humming a Guatemalan folk tune in Spanish under his breath. I heard only the lightest of whispers in the background. I could somehow sense that the gods and the priests and the audience of *fantasmas* were no longer there.

I opened my eyes and groaned. The room was still lit by fire. I was still naked on that stone slab, but I no longer shivered. I felt neither cold nor heat. I saw Carlos out of the corner of my eye. I tried to sit up, but it was too painful. Any movement at all was agonizing and exhausting. My eyes closed and I fell back into unconsciousness. For how long, I cannot say.

Some time later – minutes, hours, days? – I woke up again to find Carlos slapping my face. "Wake up, Edmundo Lopez. Wake up." I could move my head and open my eyes. His appearance was completely normal. He was wearing his blue jeans and shirt, no blue body paint, no jade mask. The whispering sound I had heard before the ritual was still all around me but now resolved into distant, distinct voices and the occasional word. Some of the torch-pots had gone out and I could smell the stale smoke of the fires from the altar that had recently been extinguished. Yet my eyes could see more clearly than when all of them had been lit. I had so many questions. But first things first.

"Water," I croaked.

He approached me in silence and poured water into my mouth. I turned my head the other way to see Pedro. Could it be? I exhaled with relief. He was breathing normally as if he were simply asleep. I heard him snore slightly. "*Mi amor,*" I whispered.

Carlos offered the first genuine smile I ever saw cross his face. "He will live, Edmundo Lopez. *La Piedra* breathes." I heard Pedro mumble something in his sleep. To hear his voice, even like this, meant the world to me.

I closed my eyes in relief. Then I tried to sit up but couldn't. "Why can't I move?"

"Your strength will return. More than you can know."

"Carlos, I had the strangest nightmare..." I took a shuddering gasp as I remembered some of the alarming fragments of the nightmare I had dreamed. I tried to move my left arm. I couldn't do it. I struggled to lift my right hand and was able to bring it to my chest. My eyes flew wide open, and I moaned. It had been no dream. I could feel the scars. Deep, thick scars. The skin and muscles of my chest had been mauled and repaired somehow. I thumped my chest. I felt not human tissue but metal. In a panic, I tried to find my pulse. I had no pulse! Nothing! Hyperventilating, I was able to lift myself up enough to rest on my arms. "My God!" I said.

"God has nothing to do with what occurred here. It was not a dream, Edmundo. Relax your breath. You no longer need so much air."

I closed my eyes. "What did you do to me?"

Carlos paused. Then he took my face into both of his hands and forced me to look at him. 'Anything' you said. Anything!" he repeated in a loud voice for emphasis. "Well, now your man lives because you have taken his place. And now you have all the gold you could ever want. Isn't that what you prayed for?"

I gasped. It was true! What I had prayed for... Yes, I had gold. But not this way! I looked over at my Pedro. How could I let him see me like this?

I breathed in deeply and found that my body required almost no breath. I was able to lift myself into a sitting position. I put both hands onto my tender chest. Then I put my hands to my ears and looked around to find the source of the whispering that sometimes resolved into individual voices - like some hideous, cacophonous choir peppered with occasional solo lines. Some of the spirits spoke in English, some in Spanish, some in a language I couldn't understand – presumably Mayan. Now I heard one child's voice crying out "Daddy..." My jaw dropped. Was that Roberto, *mi niño?* Was this what Pedro had heard? I pressed my fingers into my ears to try to smother the sounds.

I started to fall off the altar. Carlos caught me and helped me stay steady. "Those are the troubled dead," Carlos said. "They have always been there. You were not able to hear them before. Now you will never be alone."

"What the hell has happened to me?" I moaned.

"Son of my sister... there was a debt to pay. You had no choice. As for your man..." He nodded at Pedro who was sound asleep. "You said you would do anything."

I tried to rise and nearly fainted. Carlos grabbed my arm. "Lie down until the elixir wears off." I had no choice. I was still so dizzy.

"Where are my clothes?"

"Do you feel cold?"

"No, I don't feel much of anything."

"Good. You *pantalones* are here. I will bring them to you. Everything else except your backpack with the gold and your journal was burned in the fire. I took a risk on your behalf by holding these things back for you. The gods required your freedom from possessions."

"What fire?" I began to cough.

"Don't think too much, Edmundo Lopez. Have some more water."

He held the canteen for me as I drank. Then I turned to face Pedro. He was alive. He was breathing. Carlos flashed light into both of his eyes, and he made the weak mewing sound of a kitten. Carlos said Pedro would revive.

"But listen to me carefully, Edmundo Lopez. This man's mind is not strong. Were *La Piedra* to know the sacrifice you have made on his behalf it is your voice he would hear howling within his head. He would not be able to live with it. He is one who would bring harm to himself. And then your sacrifice would be for nothing."

"How can you know that?" I said hotly.

My Uncle Carlos then lifted Pedro's left wrist and ran his finger across the scar. I looked away. "And you saw with your own eyes how readily his mind deteriorated."

I could not deny the truth either of Pedro's long-ago suicide attempt or how quickly he had descended into a madness which I hoped was temporary. "So, I must never tell Pedro what happened here."

Carlos grabbed my arm. "It is more than that, *pendejo*. He must never remember that he was even here. The elixir that I gave to save his life – he will forget everything that happened here." He paused and looked down. "And *La Piedra* will forget you."

I recoiled from his words. "No, no! That's not why I did this..." I turned to Pedro's sleeping form. "Wake up, Pedro. Wake up!"

Carlos put his hand on my forehead and guided me back to a reclining position. "He will not know you. And I will not let you trouble him. You made your choice."

I could have cried but was too weak. I tried to breathe quickly but my body didn't need the air and didn't care. What I had been accused of so many times had finally become the truth: I had no heart. And I had no Pedro.

"I shall take *La Piedra* away now before he wakes up." Carlos's eyes burned into me. "You must decide now. To where shall I take him?"

The whispering voices which had been mostly silent came alive with humming sounds and occasional words. *To the temple. To the sea. To the volcano of Popocatépetl...*

I tried to shut the voices out and was slow to react. I could barely think from the physical weakness, the howling of spirits in my ears and the loss of everything that gave meaning to my life. "Take him back to El Cruce. Take some of the gold in my bag. That will pay for him to go home. Not to L.A., Carlos. He can't go back there. Send him to Florida. His aunt lives there and will welcome him. I hope."

"I do not want your gold. You have earned it. You will keep earning it for a long time to come."

"What do you mean by that?"

Carlos started to say something but then just shrugged. He started to lift Pedro and I put my hand out to stop him. "But how will you get him back to civilization?"

Carlos put Pedro back down onto the Bleeding Stone and came over to me. "While you were sleeping, the burro... she came back. Funny, huh?" He then began to chuckle.

"What's so funny?"

"Everyone gets what they want. *La Piedra* lives. You are now a rich man. Ah Puch and Buluc Chabtan are satisfied. The life of Jose Garza – that which you stole you have repaid. The rip in the fabric of the spirits is repaired." I stared at him. "Oh, and one more thing. My sister, your *madre...* she told me to tell you she is satisfied as well."

My jaw locked and my eyes dilated massively at this last statement. If there had been blood in my veins, it would have gone cold. Catrina! She had engineered everything! She knew exactly what would happen to me and that *bruja* sent me anyway. I spoke as forcefully as my weakness would allow. "You and my mother... you goddamned ghouls! Your own relative! What kind of sick retribution is this?! Why didn't you just kill me?"

He looked at me very seriously. "Ah Puch and Buluc Chabtan didn't want your life. At least not yet. *Solamente su corazón.* Just your heart. Do you not understand? Gold means very little to them while warm, pulsing flesh is everything. Don't worry, Edmundo Lopez. Now you can live as long as you like. Take of this world what you can get." He again came close to my face, grabbed both sides of my head and stared into my eyes. "And when the day comes when you finally decide you've had enough – the gold comes back here.." He released me and moved to grab his backpack. "

" *Tío* Carlos, you're not going to leave me here!"

He looked at me with neither pity nor anger. "Yes, Edmundo Lopez. I am."

I heard Pedro moan and I tried to call to him. Carlos shook his head at me. "Don't. For his sake."

As he was about to lift Pedro up Carlos hesitated. Then he came over to me and put his hand on my arm. "I never hated you, Edmundo Lopez." He looked at me intensely as if he were about to say something. He stopped himself, then ran his index finger lightly across the extensive scars on my chest. Where he touched me didn't hurt. Rather, it felt like a surge of electricity. "You are no longer merely my nephew. Now we are *hermanos*," he said. "True brothers."

The rotten bastard. And he was leaving me! And taking my Pedro with him! "Brothers?! Only if you mean Cain and Abel," I rasped. The voices whispering in my head laughed at me.

Again, he showed me that jagged grin. "*Si.* Like Cain and Abel." With both hands against my chest, he again gently pushed me backwards onto the altar. "Rest, *pendejo.* You will know when you are ready." I could scarcely struggle as he looked at me hesitantly. He then unexpectedly took hold of my right arm, bent down and kissed me hard on the lips. As he did so he placed a forceful hand below my waist, grabbed my flaccid manhood and continued to hold on to it even as his lips released mine and he looked appraisingly into my eyes.

I had experienced worse in prison, but I was outraged by this violation. He still controlled my mind in some way and, somehow, I was unable even to growl. I experienced no arousal whatsoever. After a few seconds of this, my humiliation complete, he removed his hand from my groin and lightly patted my belly. "For *La Piedra,*" he said with a soft chuckle.

He picked Pedro up as if he were as light as a pillow and walked out of the *Cuarto de Sombras.* I heard his footsteps calmly retreating down the corridor and pictured my strange uncle and my lover finally emerging from this temple of hell back out into the sunlight.

I was alone and still barely able to move. The whispering voices said *stay with us, stay!* Oh, hell no, you fucking ghosts. I spit the taste of Carlos off of my mouth. Then I slowly sat up. But when I tried to stand, blackness engulfed me. I fell, naked and unconscious, onto the hard floor of the *Templo de los Muertos.* There I stayed for days dreaming only of ghosts and jaguars.

When I finally woke up for real I could hear it raining outside. I didn't know how many days I had been unconscious but every inch of my body ached like I'd been hit by a bus. But my strength had returned. Other than a slight suspiration of whispers that I could barely discern, my head was finally clear, and I could stand and walk.

All of the torch-pots had gone out. And yet I could see in the dark. I could see as clearly as if everything emitted a faint glow. My vision had become far more acute.

I stood up and looked down at my body. I was thin and could see intense scarring on my chest. Gingerly, I tapped on my sternum and there was only the feel of metal. I felt for a heartbeat. None. I felt for my pulse. There was none. How was this possible? I was dead. Or some kind of undead. Yet I was still breathing. And I hungered. And I had to take a piss. And, above all, I thirsted. My throat was a desert from thirsting. In addition to a backpack full of gold, Carlos had left me a canteen of water and the nuts and dried pork. And my journal. I pissed on the floor in a corner. Still naked, I then ate and drank like a savage.

A savage. *Si.* I pounded my chest again and felt the metal inside of me. The emotions came pouring out of me like the storm outside. I screamed out to the voices, "What the hell am I now? What did you do to me?"

My question was answered by that ever-present suspiration of whispering voices increasing in volume as they surrounded me. "Come with us" they seemed to say. "*Vamanos.*"

"Leave me alone!" I screamed. The noise just got louder. I tried to crush my head with my hands, and it did no good. Pedro, why did I allow this? *Dios mio,* the stupid thing I had done!

I heard the creaking of a door opening. I turned to see if someone had entered the *Cuarto de Sombras* but there was no one there. It was the Treasury! That cursed, rotten treasure room. The stone door had opened by itself. Like some dead creature, I slowly walked into that room of gold pulled by this metal in my chest. That I had no flashlight or torch mattered not at all. I could see perfectly. There was a huge gold mirror on the far end of the room. Slowly I walked towards it, my features distorted like a fun-house mirror. The closer I got the more in focus my image became until I stood three feet from the mirror. Only then was I able to see fully how the Bleeding Stone had changed me.

My face looked haggard but, despite the intense sensation of having been hit by a bus, my body was intact. My head was still attached to my neck, my torso upon my hips, my muscles were all there, my hands, my navel, *mis privadas*, everything. I couldn't quite tell since the mirror itself was golden, but all I had to do was look down. My skin had a subtle gold sheen – not too obvious in the dark but I could see it. What was really visible was the scarring on my chest. There were two thick lines, each one maybe eight inches long with four smaller lines across each of the thick lines, all right over the center of my chest where my tattoo of the Sacred Heart had once rested. These scars glared red-orange and looked as if they had been slashed into my chest with barbed wire. And my normally brown eyes now had a fiery glint of gold in them. What creature of the devil had I become?

I fell onto my knees before the mirror. I was no longer human. Jesus, sweet Jesus! I had a heart made out of metal and the poison of stolen, sacred Mayan gold was infused throughout my entire body.

I curled into a fetal position in front of the mirror and moaned. I wondered if this body could still generate tears. Oh hell, yes it could. Great sobbing tears. For at least twenty minutes straight.

Eventually the tears stopped. I got up and wandered like a zombie back into the *Cuarto de Sombras*. But was I actually a dead thing? I don't know, *amigos*. I didn't know what I was. To be honest, I still don't. I only know that, despite my despair, I was starting to feel stronger. I could actually see the thinness of my arms and legs fill out into something resembling health. I tried lifting the bag filled with gold. It must have weighed about a hundred pounds. I was able to lift it with one hand. Realizing how strong I was becoming I turned my gaze over to the Bleeding Stone. Something feral filled me and I decided to topple it. But Ah Puch and Buluc Chabtan could read my thoughts and their images painted over the altar suddenly lit up brightly. The spirits were whispering *No, Mundo, you mustn't!* So, they could read my thoughts! Their whispering in my ears became such a painful hurricane of noise I had to put my hands to my ears. When I backed away from the Bleeding Stone the noise quieted to a normal level.

Despite the whispering, I noticed something else: along with my vision, my hearing had improved. I realized that I could hear what was going on outside the pyramid. That's how I knew that there was a storm raging. And, after perhaps an hour had elapsed, that's how I knew that the storm was over. That was my cue. Whatever *diablo* thing I had become, with the passing of the storm it was now time for me to leave this temple of death.

I walked over to the torch-pots next to the altar. Each one was full of ashes and the charred bits and pieces of what few possessions I had brought to Tikal. My shoes had been destroyed. Even my underwear. At least – for modesty's sake – they left me my trousers. Or so I thought. But Carlos had omitted one important fact. My trousers had been ripped into pieces and were not fit to wear. What was I supposed to do? Wander the jungles of Guatemala stark naked as I searched for a way home?

I was able to salvage part of the fabric. I tied the strips into a waistband. This way I was at least able to fashion something resembling a loin cloth. I placed this hybrid of Levi Strauss and the ancient Mayan world over my privates and returned to the mirror in the Treasury Room. I stared at the thing that Edmundo Lopez had become. I was now truly a child of the wedded Ah Puch and Buluc Chabtan.

I almost flung the loincloth off. I didn't need it. Although my gold-infused skin registered temperature, it no longer suffered from heat or cold. I could wander naked through the glaciers of Antarctica, or the steaming Amazon jungle and it would cause me no discomfort. But sooner or later I was going to encounter people. A naked man tanned slightly gold, with the scars of an angry "X" on his chest and a gold glint in his eyes was likely to raise eyebrows.

A canteen of water. Some dried food. An improvised loincloth. My journal. And a backpack full of gold. That, *amigos*, is the inventory of all that was left to me in this world.

Uncle Carlos had said that I was now a rich man. What a laugh. No amount of gold would remove these marks from my chest.

Like Cain, I was branded for all the world to see and judge.

CHAPTER 13: TO WANDER ALONE

I finally left that cursed *Templo de los Muertos* and walked out into the dappled sunlight. Of course, there was no sign of Carlos or Pedro. No burro, no supplies. I suddenly realized that my ankle no longer bothered me. Of course, that should not have surprised me in my new superhuman state. My gold-infused skin was elastic and resistant to injury. My bones had been infused with metal and were no longer susceptible to being broken. My veins and arteries no longer carried blood. And although I still hungered and thirsted, I needed only a tenth of the calories of my former life. The little bit of dried pork that I ate and the small amount of rainwater I drank would last me the entire day. I was feeling not only stronger, *amigos*, but strong. I was starting to appreciate that I was impervious to the frailties of the flesh. I hesitated, then put the pack with my stolen gold onto my back. It was not heavy in the least.

I told the voices that whispered in my ears, "Onward." The word echoed through the chorus that, I began to accept, would henceforth be my constant companions. With that, I began the long, barefoot trek south, back towards El Cruce.

I was disoriented at first. But I knew the sun rose in the east and set in the west. That told me the direction to go. What it didn't tell me was what I was going to do when I got there. I couldn't just stroll into a village like El Cruce in a loincloth, with gold-tinged skin and this massive scarring upon my chest. They would run screaming knowing me for the heartless creature of death that I had become. For that very reason I avoided the roads and wandered through the jungle like a savage. I was tortured by memories of the trek northward from El Cruce only days earlier. I remembered how the sun had burned, how I had ached with thirst and gone mad fighting mosquitos on the journey to Tikal, back in another lifetime, when Pedro and I made love and the future looked bright. Now the burning sun did nothing to my skin, I thirsted little, and the insects and other creatures of the rainforest avoided me like the plague. *Si.* That's what I was. A walking plague.

After a day and night of hiking, I came upon a rustic little farm carved out of the jungle. At this point I had no choice. If I didn't get help from someone, I would get nowhere. There was a father, a mother, a young son, a daughter, and a baby. I approached the door of their tidy little *casa* expecting them to react to me as if I were Frankenstein's monster. Close but not quite. The mother answered the door, saw me and immediately crossed herself, calling to the nearby shed "Manuel! ¡Ven aqui!" As soon as she called out she said "wait." She then closed the door on me.

The father came from behind the house and paused when he saw me. At first, he stared. Then he gestured for me to move away from the front door to the side of the house. I could see the son and daughter through the front window, their noses pressed against the glass to watch our interaction.

The father introduced himself as Manuel Zamora. I assured him that I meant no harm. That I needed help. He trembled slightly but otherwise did not betray fear of me, acting as if my appearance was no shock. But his eyes, of course, were drawn to the massive scarring on my chest. I told him my name and that my companions had abandoned me. I don't think he listened to a word I said. He just kept staring at the scar over my heart. Then, without asking, he grabbed my arm to look at its coloring. I shut up at this point and let him see fully what I was. I turned around before him so he could see all of me. He looked at me with his hands pointing at my chest as if seeking my permission to touch my scars. I nodded. He touched the scar directly over my gold heart and then recoiled. Under his breath I heard him mutter *las marcas del diablo* as he crossed himself. Finally, he looked up at me. To my shock the man had tears in his eyes. He was struggling not to weep. This, in turn, made my own eyes start to water.

"There are many terrible things in the jungle, no?" he said.

"Terrible things," I confirmed.

"You come from Tikal, do you not?" he asked.

I couldn't speak. I nodded *si* and that seemed to be all he needed to know. Manuel asked no questions either about my "tan" or the mauling of my chest. He took me by the hand and led me to the barn where he kept two goats, a mule and a cow. He had me wait there while he went back to the house to let his family know that I would be staying the night in the barn. He came back out to me and brought me some tortillas, some fruit and cold coffee. He also gave me a shirt to cover up my scars along with a pair of paint-stained trousers. He apologized that these were all they could afford to give me. They had no shoes for me. And nothing that wasn't old and soiled. I was so grateful I wanted to hug this man. But I dared not. He wouldn't have wanted that, and I could easily have crushed him to death without even trying.

His kindness moved me. What do they say? Crumbs from some may be worth more than gold from others? The gold! I remembered what I carried in my backpack and tried to give Manuel one of my gold coins. He just stared at me, shook his head, backed away from the barn crossing himself and hurried back into the house.

I was happy to spend the night with the animals in the barn. At first my presence agitated them, but I spoke to them gently and reassuringly and somehow that was enough. They soon lost their fear of me, and I felt as if I were back among the living. But I missed Pedro. And, even with a leaky roof over my head and the straw that I lay upon, I was reminded of the humanity that I had given up.

One thing I was not allowed to miss were the whispering *fantasmas* of Tikal that had come with me. But I was learning to tune them out. I fell asleep in the straw. This time I dreamt not of ghosts but of Tikal as the vibrant, cultured city of the Maya that it must have been back in the day. I heard the voices of costermongers selling corn and beans. I heard laughter and the shouts of children at play. I saw the pyramids of the Lost World and they were new, stately and beautifully colored red and green. I did not consider the horrific events that occurred within their walls. Why let a little human sacrifice ruin a perfect urban adventure, right *amigos?*

I ended up staying with Manuel Zamora and his family for three days as I continued to strengthen and acclimatize. The children were fascinated by me – they rarely met strangers – and Manuel simply told them that I was an explorer who had gotten lost in the jungle. They did not know enough to be startled by the subtle coloring in my skin. But Manuel's wife, Lupe, certainly did. She wanted nothing to do with me and crossed herself every time she saw me. She would not allow me in their *casa*, nor could I eat with them. Of all the family, she was the only one to treat me as if I were a leper.

I am many heartless things, *amigos*, but you should also know that I am a man who pays his debts. Since Manuel would not accept gold, I helped him plough his fields. I had been a strong man long before I became the property of Ah Puch and Buluc Chabtan. But now I was strong enough to lift a horse. I spent that third day helping Manuel and his son prepare the fields. It was back-breaking work in such a hot, humid climate, but I never even broke a sweat.

I could have stayed at the Zamora farm for another few days. But then the place in my chest where my heart used to be started to ache for Pedro. It was time for me to move on. Lupe was relieved. I think Manuel was, too, although he was nothing but kind to me. He had an old pick-up truck and knew the back way to El Cruce. He drove me the thirty miles or so from the farm to the village. When we got to within a mile of El Cruce he let me out. He did not say it, but I think he did not want the people of the village to know that he was associated with me. I also now knew enough not to insult him with an offer of any of the Mayan gold. I reached out my hand to him not knowing if he would accept it or not. He did. He then grasped my shoulder with the other hand and wished me well. He made the sign of the cross over me – that quieted the whispering voices in my ear for a full five minutes – and then he drove off.

There were tears in my eyes as I watched him drive away. There are tears in my eyes now as I write this, *amigos*. I will never forget Manuel Zamora's kindness. He helped to make up for the horror that was my Uncle Carlos. In hindsight, his gentle kindness reminded me of Magdalena, Pedro's sister – the lover who once bore me a son. The lover and the *niño* whose lives I ruined because of the curse I had brought upon us all. Well, now I was paying that debt.

I was afraid to enter the town. I was a monster, inside and out. I beat my hand against the metal in my chest and cried, wondering if I would ever be forgiven.

It took me 20 minutes to hike into El Cruce. It had been less than two weeks since Pedro, Carlos and I had walked away from this little *pueblo*. It felt like an entire lifetime for me. Everything in my life had been altered. I was ashamed of what I had become. And yet upon my back I carried a fortune in gold. By my calculation, the equivalent of $800,000. in U.S. dollars. Maybe that doesn't sound like a lot to you, *amigos*, but trust me. It was more money than I could ever have conceived. And besides... well, I'll explain that part later.

As soon as I got to El Cruce, I avoided the villagers and went directly to Carlos's house. Nobody was home. The front door was unlocked so I walked in. The place was stripped empty except for the furniture. There was nothing here, no artifacts, no clothing. Oh, except for a pair of shoes and socks that were on the floor by his bedroom. Although I had gotten used to being barefoot, I knew I would be facing the people of this village sooner rather than later, so I put them on.

Then I walked to the little plaza and randomly started asking the villagers if they had seen Carlos or Pedro. Gone. Both gone. Carlos had abandoned his house and fields and disappeared *"con el Americano"* without a trace. The people I questioned – how they stared at me! Was it the gold glint in my eyes? They couldn't see the scar over my heart since it was now covered by Manuel's long-sleeved shirt. But did it matter?

I went back into Carlos's house. I looked at my face in the mirror. There was no question that it betrayed the loss of my human heart. Despite the glint of gold, I was dead behind the eyes. Then, I noticed that there was an envelope addressed to me on the kitchen table. I tore it open and read:

Dear Edmundo,

Now that the debt for Jose Garza has been paid, I am free to leave El Cruce. I will not play games with you. I am taking La Piedra to Miami in the USA just as you have requested. I do not want you to follow us. And just in case you are wondering, I am not taking La Piedra for myself. My interests lie in a different direction. It is possible, my nephew, that our paths will cross again. You will decide if and when the time comes. I have left El Cruce for now so that I can see some of the world that you, Catrina and Pedro have seen. But I will be back. When you decide that you want to see me again – I have no doubt that you will, pendejo – I will be back. Until then, you are free. Enjoy your gold. And you need never again pretend that you have a heart.

Tío Carlos

The rotten bastard! Heartless! *He* called *me* heartless. The ghosts whispering in my ears reached an unexpected crescendo. I dropped the letter onto the floor and howled in agony. A passer-by knocked on the door to make sure I was alright but when she saw me her eyes bugged out and she hurried away, crossing herself. After being treated with kindness and respect by Manuel Zamora, I now felt more alone than I could ever have imagined.

There was one other thing that I found at Carlos's house – hidden behind the toolshed was the used Ford I had bought in Puerto San José. This much Carlos had left me, much to my surprise. I had assumed that when he took Pedro away and emptied his house, he would have taken *el carro* as his transportation. I still have no idea how my Uncle and my lover left El Cruce. When I asked the villagers, they said that Carlos and the foreigner were there one day and in the morning they were gone. Yet another mystery in this strange place.

I walked all around that car. Forgetting my new powers, I kicked the tires and the whole car moved. I had to be careful. I still didn't know my own strength. But I certainly knew my weakness. Maybe this was where my family was from. Maybe this was where I was born, but I did not belong here. I didn't know where on this green Earth I belonged, but I knew for damned sure that it wasn't here in El Cruce.

I was ready to leave. I had some things on my list of assets. Though now undead, I was strong, resilient and still handsome as the devil. I had transportation and a bag which carried a fabulous amount of wealth. Except for the chorus of agonized whispers that haunted me day and night, I was free.

Free. Well, at least that's what some of you might think, *mis amigos*

CHAPTER 14: LOS ANGELES

At first, I thought to return to the port and see if I could book passage on a ship. But to where? To remain in Guatemala was out of the question, but I didn't know any place in this world except the streets of L.A. Home. I therefore decided to drive from Guatemala all the way to the U.S.A. By being in the driver's seat of my own car, I could keep my distance from others. El Cruce was near the Mexican border. I figured I would enter the Yucatan and then drive clear across Mexico, from the Caribbean to the Pacific. I would then dump the car in Tijuana and find a way to sneak across the border into San Diego. From there I could take the train up to L.A.

My plan worked like a charm with only a few incidents in which people were suspicious of my strange appearance. I took care to wear only long pants and long-sleeved shirts. I even grew a beard. With some women's cosmetics on my face hardly anybody who came into contact with me was any the wiser. The biggest problem was the color of my eyes which glittered no matter what I did. So, I stole a pair of sunglasses and, for the most part, that did the trick.

The other problem was keeping people from guessing what filled my backpack. After I crossed into Mexico, I purchased two bags made of strong leather. That did the trick. Nobody bothered me. That is until I reached Veracruz. That's when I was attacked by *banditos*. They didn't see the leather bags I had stashed under my car seats. All that they saw was that I was sleeping in my car in the outskirts of the city. They thought they could steal my car, take my wallet and anything else I might have of value and if I ended up dead no one would know the difference. Well, *amigos*, there were five of these tough guys, all in their 20s, reeking of tequila and beer. Among these five there were three guns, two knives and a lot of fists. And by the time I was done with them, there were three broken legs, five broken arms and at least two of them will never have children. They were lucky that I let them live. But you could hear their macho sobs halfway to Puebla. And during that melee I never even broke a sweat.

Something new appeared in my eyes that night. A spark of Buluc Chabtan, the god of war, perhaps. Whatever it was, it was something menacing in my eyes, my posture, my face that made people avoid confronting me. I was never threatened again. "Pedro," I whispered, as I drove on to Mexico City. "I'm glad you don't have to see me this way."

A week later I was in Tijuana – a town I knew only too well. This was the border, a city famous for its underworld. To an *hombre* like me, it was like coming home.

Despite having no passport or identification of any kind, I was able to make it over the border into the U.S. and back to Los Angeles. It wasn't hard. I had spent years as a smuggler, remember? I had contacts in both TJ and San Diego. Whether it's in the real estate business, the entertainment industry or among the smugglers of the street, business connections matter.

Back in California I worried that my monstrous nature would be discovered, and I'd be arrested or come to the attention of some mad scientist who might want to study me. I needn't have worried. This was Los Angeles, after all. In a city full of actors, make-up artists, and avant garde performers, my subtle gold "tan" and glittering eyes rarely raised eyebrows. With some cash directed to the right people, there was no problem acquiring a new name and a new identity. The right clothes and make-up covered a multitude of inconvenient questions. And I found a way to rebuild my life – whatever that meant with respect to a handsome, dead thing like me.

So, *amigos*. Do you want to know how to rebuild your life with two leather satchels full of Mayan gold? Pay attention.

First, you use your underworld connections to have anything of archaeological merit sold on the black market.

Second, you use your other underworld connections to have your priceless Mayan gold coins and other artisanal objects melted down into untraceable ingots.

Next, you take the cash you receive in exchange and you buy a small piece of land in the San Fernando Valley. A piece of land that your connections tell you will soon be needed by the County of Los Angeles for one reason or another. You sell that land for double what you paid for it. You use that money to buy a duplex. You flip it. Then you buy an apartment building. You keep that because the rental income starts to outweigh the Mayan gold you still keep locked up in your safe. You buy, and you sell, and you buy. Sooner than you can imagine, you own a substantial percentage of Los Angeles County, with some interests as well in Orange County and Palm Springs. Before you know it, you – a poor boy from the back streets of L.A. – have accountants and brokers and lawyers on retainer.

You're fabulously rich and who the hell cares?

The voices whispering in my ears sure didn't care. They still don't. The litany of people whose death I had caused one way or the other didn't care. And the man I wanted to become rich for -- Pedro, *mi amor*

– was alive somewhere but lost to me forever.

Maybe you'll appreciate the irony, *amigos*. Love was dead to me, and wealth now meant little. I had the Midas touch. The gold I had smuggled into the U.S. was a fraction of what I was able to earn through its use as seed money. But I longed for a life that didn't just revolve around wealth.

Remember how I told you that when I was a young boy, I kept a journal and wrote stories? And remember that I even kept a journal going into Tikal? Well, that desire to write and tell stories is also something I was able to turn into gold. Since love was out of the question, I followed the only dream left to me and pursued a career writing for Hollywood's entertainment industry. I still have to laugh. The "industry" is a world where not having a heart is a distinct advantage. I look out my penthouse window at the traffic going east and west on Hollywood and Sunset Boulevards. I don't have to see people. I sit at a computer and write under a bunch of pseudonyms.

You have almost certainly heard of me, but I will not connect the dots for you. Most of the time I write what I like, though I occasionally type out the agonies described by the Tikal *fantasmas* who haunt me. Depending on which pseudonym I'm using on a given day my words get used in commercials, YouTube, cable television, *telenovelas* or Academy Award winning films. Under certain well-known pen names, I've been nominated for three Oscars. I haven't won any yet, *amigos*, but who knows? You hear performers speak my words all the time without being the least bit aware your entertainments are written by a heartless monster from El Cruce who once killed a man of unexpected importance, who loved just one other man – a gentle one – a long time ago, who slogged his way through more than one jungle, and who gave up his life for gold.

By the way, don't think I just take dictation from the Tikal spirits. I have my own stories to tell. Though, truth be known, those lousy ghosts do sometimes inspire me in the worst possible way. At first, I thought they'd make me lose my mind, but you know me – I'm resilient. Some people have tinnitus. I have *los fantasmas de Tikal.* You get used to them. When it comes to human contact, they're what's left to me. Especially the one who calls me "Daddy."

Why they follow me I can't say. At the peak of when they were driving me mad and I yearned to rip out my eardrums, I spoke anonymously with an anthropology professor from the University in Mexico City. I told him I was a screenwriter who needed insight on a picture I was working on. So, he proposed this theory: the Mayan object in my chest is a sort of portal between the world of the unhappy dead and the world of the unhappy living. First *las fantasmas* sought out Pedro. Then when I took his place they attached themselves to me. That doesn't explain why *el niño*, baby Roberto, follows me but when all is said and done, he's the only relative I've got who cares for me. There's nothing I can do to silence them.

Well, there's one thing I could do. But that would require me to go back to Tikal. That's what I'm thinking I want to do. But I'm scared.

They're calling to me right now, even as I write on this computer. "*Ayuda me*" one says. Help me. "*Da me su corazon.*" Give me your heart. Too late. Been there, done that.

There's one thing I'm grateful for though: Pedro's voice isn't among them. He got away. My Pedro got away.

Alright, *amigos.* Now you know everything about how I went to Tikal and lost my heart. And my Pedro. Forever.

It's not completely terrible. I do rather enjoy being rich. Very rich. You won't find the name Edmundo Lopez in any of the property records, but through a set of clever closely-held corporations I own a surprisingly large chunk of California. As for my career as a writer – now you can understand that I don't need the money. It's a hobby, not a necessity. But I do like to write entertainments! I love those Spielberg movies. And old epics like Ben Hur and Spartacus. But don't ask me to watch The Wizard of Oz. The yearning faced by the Tin Man hits far too close to home.

Movies are a blast. Putting words on paper gives me something to do. And putting words in peoples' mouths gives me satisfaction.

I must confess that I do get lonely. I'm stronger than any human you'll ever meet, but what does it matter? Like a vampire, I only go out at night when my subtle gold sheen looks like no more than a chemical tan. I wear long-sleeve shirts, I put contact lenses in my eyes. Once in a while I go out to the bars. I can drink but I can't get drunk. I never pick up men. Or women. I have no blood and, therefore, neither the ability to have an erection nor even residual sexual desire. To be honest, *amigos*, I haven't experienced sexual arousal since I was with Pedro the night before Tikal. I don't even have friends. If it wasn't for the Tikal voices, Facebook and Instagram, I'd be completely alone. You think that's messed up? Let me tell you something even more messed up. I don't age. I can't even die. Believe me, I've tried in about two dozen different ways.

As for the aging part... I haven't told you when the events in my story took place. I was afraid you wouldn't believe me. But if you're with me this far, *amigos*... well... here goes. Pedro, my Uncle Carlos and I arrived at Tikal in October of 1922. Pancho Villa was still roaming the byways of Chihuahua. Warren Harding was president. Movies were silent, Clara Bow was It. Oh, and the illegal product that I used to smuggle into the U.S.? It was tequila from Mexico. This was during Prohibition. I was born in 1891. That means that I'm over 130 years old. I still look like a good-looking *hombre* of 30 with a slight gold tan, but who the hell cares?

October 30, 1922. That was the day I lost my heart in Tikal. November 2, 1922. That's the date I rose up from unconsciousness after Carlos took Pedro and left me in that damned temple, naked and too weak to move. Ironically, that was the Day of the Dead. I haven't aged a single day since. I'd like to tell you I can't weep, but that wouldn't be true. I still thirst and my tear ducts work perfectly – a male version of *La Llorona*. I register hot and cold but they give me no discomfort. I register emotion but it's mostly cold and heartless, like this metal in my chest.

Actually, that's not completely true. Even after one hundred years, I still feel warmth when I think of Pedro. I feel grateful that he didn't die in that pit of horrors with his soul in torment. I rescued him from that and took his suffering upon myself. Pedro was four years younger than me – he was born in 1895. He died in 1978. Once he was freed from the gods and spirits of Tikal – and me – he had a good long life.

I have also had a long life. If you could call it living. I watched silent films transition into talkies. I held my fortune through the Great Depression (what could be safer than gold in a safe?) I was never called into service during World War II because I was too old – and Uncle Sam didn't have my real name anyway. On and on the years went. A group of scientists in Los Alamos invented nuclear weapons. Then there was television, then satellites. Before I knew it, people were protesting the Vietnam War, cooking with microwave ovens and walking on the moon. Jazz passed into swing, rock and roll, then disco.

Speaking of disco, I walked into a discotheque in West Hollywood in 1976 and, for the first time in decades, felt like I fit in somewhere. My skin was gold and so was half the room. I remember drinking whiskey sours and pretending I could get drunk, even though I couldn't. I remember a trio of girls with hair dyed pink and purple coming on to me. Remember, *amigos*, that I'm still 30 and handsome as the devil.

And then in a far corner of the room – past all the dancers – I saw him. A man with olive skin and a thin mustache who looked for all the world like Pedro. The music receded into silence. The chunk of metal in my chest couldn't skip a beat, but it sure felt like it was vibrating. Time stood still for me at that moment. I walked right across the dance floor threading my way through all those Travolta-Bee-Gee wannabees gyrating under the strobe lights and mirror ball. I went right up to this handsome man who was sitting all by himself at a small table.

"You look like someone I used to know," I said.

The guy flashed a sexy smile. "Great pick-up line. Maybe he's a relative. Try me."

"Pedro," I said. "Pedro Luna."

"Doesn't ring any bells. I'm Abel." He put his hand out for me to shake and when I did, he pressed one or two fingers into my palm suggestively. His liquid brown eyes looked as if they saw right through my clothes. "Abel," he repeated softly. "And you're damned cute. But I have to tell you that I'm here with my boyfriend."

At that moment a tall blond anglo dude carrying two margaritas interrupted us. I bowed in deference to their relationship and walked away. But as I turned to leave the disco, I saw Abel gazing at me intensely. Boyfriend or not, he was cruising me. I smiled sadly to myself and walked out. A hundred years ago, that would have meant something to me.

I walked to where I had parked my car. I was in no hurry and walked the long way parallel to Santa Monica Boulevard so I could look up at the moon. Then I drove my 1976 Maserati back to my oh-so-expensive art-deco high-rise and took my private elevator up to the penthouse. I grabbed the gold statuette of a jaguar that I kept next to my desk and moved as if to throw it through the window. Then I held it tightly in my hand as I stared out at the glitter that was the City of Angels until the dawn broke. Only then did the whispering voices in my head finally sing me to sleep.

Over the course of the next few weeks, I spent a lot of time walking in the neighborhood around my condo — mostly at night. I wandered aimlessly down Gower to Sunset Boulevard, over to Cahuenga, once or twice up Beachwood all the way to the Hollywood sign. I was simply killing time, putting off the pilgrimages I knew I had to make. Finally, it was time and I decided to look for the building where I lived when Catrina died, right before Tikal. It had been a ramshackle building with apartments smaller than my penthouse bathroom. But it was a place where I lived a human life, where I got drunk and wrote stories. It was a place where I used to make love with many partners. Handsome men. A few lovely women. Magdalena. Pedro. Now when I went to the old address, I saw that this shitty old building wasn't there anymore. It was replaced by a strip mall.

As I stood there in front of the 7-Eleven staring at the now-lost location where so much of my past had taken place, a young dude came up to me. Latino. Late teens, muscle shirt. Track marks on his arms. "Nice tan," he said. I said thank you. Then he let me know what he charged for a dizzying array of sexual favors. I just shook my head. Not this time. Not ever. But as I started to leave, I got curious and asked him what his name was. "Pedro," he answered. *Ay.* I handed him a twenty and gave him a pat on the shoulder as I left.

Amigos, I must tell you the truth. Once I had that encounter at the 7-11, I could no longer stand not knowing — not even for one more day.

In January of 1977 – 55 years or so after Tikal – I hired a private detective with contacts in Florida. At last, I learned all about my one-time lover. Pedro Luna was alive. And, in response to some fancy questioning which involved a non-existent probate related to my non-existent death, my investigator learned that – contrary to what Carlos had predicted -- Pedro remembered me. But not fondly. Somehow, he had been led to believe that I had abandoned him somewhere in Florida back in his youth. Thanks, Uncle Carlos. *Pendejo.*

The report I got from Letat Investigations gave me all of the details that I didn't want to know and yet desperately craved. Here's a summary:

Rewind to the early 1920s. Apparently it didn't take long for Pedro to get over me. After having overcome some type of brain injury which affected his memory, Pedro's vigor was restored at a mental hospital in Fort Lauderdale in early 1923. He attended school and went on to become an elementary school teacher. Pedro fell in love with a good man – an airplane mechanic named Oscar Salazar – a Cuban dude – sometime in 1924. They lived in Miami. They had a happy partnership even though there was no such thing as gay marriage in those days.

It was hard for me to read all this. If we had never gone to Tikal, if I had somehow gotten my act together, if I'd never killed Jose Garza, that happy partnership could have been us!

The relationship between Pedro and Salazar ended when Salazar died from lung cancer in the late 1960s. But here's where things get interesting. Salazar had been a widower when he and Pedro met. He had two little boys to raise after his wife died from influenza. (Believe it or not, people actually died of the flu in those days, *amigos.*) Pedro became second father to those boys and, by all accounts, a good and loving one who was completely committed to his adopted family. In fact, my investigator found a letter in the Salazar probate file that called Pedro Luna "the heart of the family." There were other witness testaments which supported Pedro inheriting 50% of the Salazar estate, the same as if he and Oscar had been legally married. There was no denying that Pedro was sincerely loved by Oscar's children. By *their* children.

Ay amigos... I cursed and pounded the metal in my chest wondering why it couldn't crack into a hundred pieces.

By coincidence, their oldest was a boy named Roberto. Roberto Salazar. My private investigators found a picture of him. He was a good looking fellow. I wondered fleetingly if he was gay, but what does it matter? Either way, he died a hero at Normandy on June 6, 1944.

Pedro and Oscar's other son was named Matthew. Matthew became a lawyer, got married sometime around 1950 and had a couple of kids himself – Pedro's grandchildren. Those kids are now in their sixties and have children of their own, Pedro's great-grandchildren. My Pedro had a good and full life with a man who loved him, children, grandchildren, great grandchildren. He did well for someone who started out as a cheap street hustler in the back alleys of Hollywood who had nowhere to go but down.

I've told you that this gold-infused body I inhabit still allows tears. Well, *amigos*, here they come.

You must understand something. There were times when I desperately wanted to contact Pedro but stayed away. Uncle Carlos had been right about that one thing. It was for Pedro's own good. What would he have done with a heartless man like me saddled with a cohort of ever-present depressed ghosts and living on wealth borrowed from the Mayan gods of death and war? I would have been poison for him.

So, along with details like social security information and fifty years worth of addresses, Letat Investigations gave me details on how to find him now. I was torn. Should I? Shouldn't I? I thought about how strange it was meeting Pedro's doppelganger, Abel, at the disco. I stared into the mirror. I reread my Tikal journal from 1922.

I picked up the small golden jaguar statuette that I kept on my desk and placed it against my cheek, then pressed it against the scars which protected this lump of metal in my chest. I finally decided that my in-human suffering through these many decades justified a visit.

CHAPTER 15: FLORIDA

I flew to Florida in May, 1978. Don't laugh at me, amigos. It was the first time I was ever in an airplane, and I was terrified the entire trip there. I didn't fly PanAm or TWA because I couldn't risk getting too close to people under that artificial light. You can get away with a little gold sheen at the discotheque or on the decadent streets of Hollywood, but not in too many other places. So, I chartered a private plane and paid the pilot handsomely to ask no questions.

I rented a car in Miami and stayed overnight in one of those fancy art deco hotels just to check out Miami Beach. I'd heard a lot about the gay scene there. It didn't disappoint. Boy were things different than in the late 1910s and 20s!

The next morning, I rented a TransAm, drove through the famous Everglades and up the Gulf Coast to Tampa. That's where Pedro's nursing home, Coral Palms, was. I bought flowers before I arrived. Then I checked in at the front desk and identified myself as one of Pedro Luna's grandkids. The humorless nurse looked me up and down with a sour face and said, "nice tan." Then she directed me to room 212. They phoned him to let him know I was on my way.

If I had had a heart, it would have been beating madly.

I knocked on the door. Twenty seconds later Pedro answered.

I hid my shock. The elderly man who stood before me... his hair was white, his skin was thin like parchment. He was clearly ill. I had seen men his age who were far more robust. This old man had the look of someone struggling with cancer. But I could see my Pedro's beauty underneath despite the years. The scar on his face had softened into a wrinkle. His eyes were still kind though they now contained something else – confidence, perhaps. The confidence of one who does not gladly suffer fools.

I was paralyzed as I stood in the doorway of his room and stared into this old man's face.

He didn't recognize me. "Well?" he grunted.

The voice was deeper, more gravelly than I had remembered. I apologized and entered. Then I handed him the bouquet of roses. He seemed puzzled to receive them. He put them on a shelf without a thank you or any kind of sentimental reaction.

I hid my hurt. I had made a grave mistake coming here. What had I hoped to accomplish?

He was very direct with me. "They told me you were one of my grandsons. But I don't know you."

"They made a mistake, Pe...Mr. Luna. I'm not your grandson. I'm the grandson of someone you might not remember."

"Try me. What was his name?"

I studied his face carefully as I answered. "His name was Edmundo Lopez."

Silence as Pedro's mouth opened and then closed again. He seemed confused by this visit from a man with a light gold tan who looked like he was in his 30s. But then I could see that "aha" moment in his eyes and they went from dull to glimmering. "Edmundo? You mean Mundo?" I simply nodded. "Your *abuelo*?" I nodded again just once. His eyes grew wide and he reached for his glasses. He put them on and stared at me. He had to have known who I was! I could see it in his eyes. I had wondered if he'd recognize me. The *fantasmas* of Tikal, who had been murmuring in the background began to whisper more loudly as Pedro and I gazed at each other. Those spirit parasites were still drawn to him. I had to be careful not to give them any encouragement.

Pedro continued to gaze at me, and I gazed back. The last time I had seen him he had been unconscious and slung over *Tío* Carlos's shoulder as they left me abandoned in the *Templo de los Muertos* at the mercy of Ah Puch and Buluc Chabtan. And the last time Pedro saw me was before the transformation, before he insanely jumped into that pit of skeletons at the base of the pyramid and struck his head. I looked a bit different then. My muscles weren't quite so filled out as they were now. I didn't have this subtle gold sheen. My eyes didn't have this amber glint. I had no heart, but did I ever? Despite my transformation in Tikal, I was still recognizably Mundo.

Pedro kept staring at me. Was he making an inventory of these changes? Could he tell that I was no longer human? And yet my face was the same. My hair, my mustache, every expression of my face would have been exactly what he remembered from the days when Warren Harding was still president.

"Come here, Mundo's grandson." He gestured with a claw-like hand. I complied and sat in the chair next to his. Pedro's voice was not only deeper; it was unquestionably more assertive. He had been a mostly immature, somewhat nellie young man when we had been lovers. He had been as sexually experienced as any street hustler would be, but emotionally immature. But that had been two to three generations earlier. Between 1922 and 1978 Pedro had lived out an entire lifetime of work and relationships and challenges and grief. He had raised children and buried one. He, too, had lived through the Great Depression, World War II, the nuclear age. And through it all he had grown and grown. I, on the other hand, had stopped my emotional growth at the age of 31. I must confess, *amigos*, that the amount of life-experience this old version of Pedro had acquired was intimidating to me.

"Do you have a name?" he asked me.

I tried to think of a lie quickly. The first name that came to my mind was Roberto, but to identify myself with our dead son would have been unspeakably cruel.

"I asked you, young man, if you have a name?"

"Ed," I answered. It was the truth.

"Ed," he repeated. "Of course it is." Then, without asking permission Pedro lifted my hand and studied it. I had a scar on that hand from a knife fight in prison before Tikal. He frowned and muttered something to himself. Clearly, he remembered. And he stared at my skin as if he understood the source of its gold sheen. He rubbed at it slightly, probably to see if it would rub off. "*Dios mio*" he muttered to himself. He put his hand on my face. No human soul had touched my face in 56 years. I trembled at the touch of Pedro's skin. I could have died content at that moment – if only I could die. And still I said nothing.

He was silent for several minutes. He pulled his hand back from my face and placed it on the table. His fingers tapped the yellow and green formica. After a few moments he removed his glasses and asked me point blank. "Why have you come here?"

I wasn't sure if I should keep up the charade or tell the truth. Believe it or not, I did something I had never once done since Tikal. I silently asked the *fantasmas* what they thought. There was a sudden hush and in that silence the thought occurred to me that the whole point of everything that I had done was to spare Pedro this supernatural burden that had been imposed on me by Ah Puch and Buluc Chabtan and Jose Garza and Carlos Lopez...

"Why have you come here?" he repeated. I understood the silence of the Mayan ghosts. Say nothing. I therefore did what came naturally and lied. But I didn't do that for my benefit. I did it for Pedro. Let him die in peace, the silence suggested. And so, I lied and told him simply that he was mentioned in my grandfather's journal – that I wanted to meet him for myself.

"And what did your *abuelo* say about me?" There was an eagerness in his voice which pleased me very much.

I looked him squarely in the eyes. "He said that you were Edmundo's one and only true love."

Pedro sighed deeply. His tears welled as he looked deep into my gold-flecked eyes. He got up and, using his cane, walked over to the window. From there he croaked the words "My Mundo." Pedro then turned to face me. "Once I thought Edmundo Lopez was *un hombre sin corazón* – a man with no heart. But I was wrong. No one has ever loved me like he did."

"No one, *Señor* Luna," I affirmed.

"Call me Pedro." He came back and sat with me at the table. "So, Ed, you refer to Mundo in the past tense - as if he is not alive."

I fidgeted until I could find the right words. "He is no longer alive – to anything that ever mattered to him."

Although this answer must have surprised him, he nodded imperceptibly. He took my hand and traced the scar that was on it. "I see, Ed. *Veo todo*" he said, speaking in Spanish as he sometimes did when we used to be together. *I see everything.*

He patted my hand and then shocked the hell out of me with his next question. "Would you like to see a photograph?"

Wait, what? I nodded curiously. What photograph? And then to my great shock Pedro reached into the desk drawer next to his chair and pulled out an old sepia colored photograph and handed it to me. It was now his turn to study my reaction.

I looked at it for a moment and then caught my breath. The *fantasmas* of Tikal whispering in my ears made room for *el niño*, the one who called me "Papa." This photograph depicted Pedro Luna, Magdalena Luna and a man of ordinary flesh and blood who was once called Edmundo Lopez. These three young people, so untouched, so innocent, were posed at a photography studio, typical of the late 1910s. Magdalena sat on a small ottoman with Pedro and me standing behind her. I gasped as I remembered where and when this photograph was taken. It had been on Sunset Boulevard back in L.A. It was in 1918 just after World War I had ended. How did Pedro get this photograph? When he had left Tikal he had no possessions but the clothes on his back. Carlos had taken him to live with his aunt Josefina in Florida and...ah. That's why I had never seen this picture before. Pedro had mailed this picture to his aunt back in 1918, shortly before I killed Jose Garza and went to prison, long before Magdalena's death and long before Pedro and I ever went to Guatemala. No wonder we looked so young, so untouched by the corrosion that the challenges of life can inflict.

I noted how worn and wrinkled this photograph was. I was deeply moved. It was in the top drawer of Pedro's desk and had obviously been looked at a thousand times. I could feel Pedro's eyes on me as I stared at this photograph depicting three people who loved each other so imperfectly over a hundred years ago. *Ay,* my eyes began to well up. It took all of my Frankenstein-like strength not to weep, *amigos.* If I could have, I would have sobbed like a child in front of this old man who had once been my lover. I could have destroyed furniture and torn the door from its hinges. But to keep oneself from sobbing? That's harder.

I looked up at Pedro and saw such kindness in his eyes. I remembered how bright those eyes were in the Guatemalan rainforest. How full those lips were, how eagerly his flesh pressed into mine. This old man, so ill, so desiccated – I was desperate for him to take me in his arms and tell me that everything would be alright. Instead, I coughed and tried not to choke. He could see my struggle. He patted me on the arm and said "there, there."

I wanted to tell him everything – everything that had happened to me. It was like floodwaters pressing against a weakening dam. But I didn't. I couldn't. The one and only reason Pedro had had a rich and full life was because I had stayed away.

I caught my breath, stood up and faced away from him. It was my turn to look out the window. There were palm trees and birds of paradise. There was a gardener riding a mower across the grass and some elderly people playing cards at a picnic table. On a table next to Pedro's window I noticed a little pile of medical supplies. I turned around and looked at my old lover again, this time really looking at him. The scar he had from that trick gone wrong back in 1917 was still there. He was thinner than I had ever seen him. This old man probably weighed 130-140 pounds. Pedro used to have strong arms, not heavily muscled like mine, but lean, sexy. Now they were parchment paper with blue veins and bruises from where he had received chemotherapy. He had a slight tremor. For the first time ever, I felt lonely and abandoned when the Tikal *fantasmas* gave me a break and became hard to hear.

I went to him. I kneeled beside Pedro, *mi amor*, and took his hand and asked him if he felt alright, if there was anything I could get him.

"Anything that I needed from you I received long ago," he said. "And, of course, from your... *abuelo*." He now looked into my eyes with great seriousness. "If Mundo were here, I'd thank him in person." He patted my arm then grabbed it with a shockingly strong grip. "What I learned about Mundo in time was that underneath it all, despite every problem we ever had, despite every adventure and misadventure, he had *un corazón de oro* – a heart of gold." At this point he let go of my arm. He reached over to my face and tilted my chin so that I would have to look at him. He looked at me hard in the eyes. "Edmundo Lopez saved me." He then let go of my chin, closed his eyes and settled back in his chair. "He saved my life. More importantly, he saved my soul."

Jesus, did Pedro really say that? That I had saved him? Oh, *amigos*. He did. I had to excuse myself and go to the restroom so that he wouldn't see the tears streaming down my gold-tinted face from my amber-tinted eyes. I cried like I did that day in Tikal when I lay sobbing, naked on the floor of the *Templo de los Muertos* mourning the fact that I was no longer human. Now, for the first time in a hundred years, I felt like maybe I still was. Just a little.

When I got back to his room, it was time for Pedro's pills and a nap. Before I left, he had me bend my ear to his mouth so he could whisper to me. "You think I don't know. I may be a sick old man, but I'm not a fool. I know that it's you, Mundo. I've always known that you were still alive. I never forgot you. I know what you did for me. Your Uncle Carlos told me. Once I was myself again, I made him tell me about everything that happened in that horrible pyramid. What you took upon yourself was beyond belief. But he told me to never seek you out or it would destroy you. I knew he was right. But I never forgot you. Edmundo Lopez, you were always *mi verdadero amor* – my true love." He pulled my head to him and then kissed me on the forehead, slowly as if he were a parent blessing a child.

"And you mine," I whispered softly.

"I want you to see something," he said. He stood up, held onto my arm and had me walk him over to the wall behind the television. There were a number of photographs hung. He pointed them out with pride. Pictures with Oscar Salazar. Their two children, "Robbie and Matt." Photos of children and grandchildren ranging from the sepia of the 1920s all the way to the color polaroids popular in the 70s. Pedro faced me and put his hand on my chest as if we were lovers once again. He pressed it in two or three places as if to satisfy himself that I had no heartbeat. He started to speak but couldn't. After two or three more tries, he looked up at me with tears in his eyes. "I lived my life for the two of us," Pedro said. I took his hand and kissed it. He then took both of our joined hands and placed them against his cheek.

As I started to leave, he again surprised me. "I want you to kiss me one last time, Mundo."

I looked at him. He was an old man, frighteningly thin and frail with chemotherapy bruises on his arms and the beginnings of a cataract in his right eye. I had no lust within this heartless, gold-infused body and Pedro's good looks were but a geriatric shadow of what they had once been. But he was my Pedro and one kiss from him was worth all the gold and jade in the world.

I gently took him in my arms and placed my lips against his and kissed him the way lovers kiss. Our kiss lasted for half a minute or more. I released him and looked deeply into his eyes. Then, without any further words between us, I left. Dry-eyed because all tears had been spent, I drove back to Miami. I flew home to Los Angeles that very night.

I heard that Pedro died about a month after that.

That was over forty years ago.

I'm still here.

CHAPTER 16: EL PROMETEO MODERNO

They say, "time waits for no man." Well, I'm no longer a man so how in hell does that apply to me? For me time waits. And waits. And waits.

The 1980s pass. Ronald Reagan. AIDS. Glasnost. Then the 90s when I bought my first personal computer, joined something called the World Wide Web and avidly followed news of Bill Clinton and the fellatio that was heard around the world. The turn of the Millenium. The Y2K virus which never came. Years of Bush Junior. 9/11. The 2010s. Obama, HBO, iPads and smartphones, Trump, and a pandemic disease that cannot touch me. Think of it, *amigos*! I was born before the Wright Brothers flew their first plane; before radio existed. When I was in my twenties, I thought Irving Berlin and George Gershwin were about as hip and syncopated as you could get. And now? My ears are assaulted with music I can no longer understand or enjoy, and which makes the whispering *fantasmas* of Tikal sound better and better.

I like your movies, though. And your 500-channel flat-screen televisions. And I especially like your cars. Cars in the 21st Century – especially the expensive ones – beat the hell out of that old Model T I drove from El Cruce to Tijuana back in 1922.

Time waits and waits and suddenly it's the 2020s. I remember looking in the mirror on New Year's Day of 2023 looking exactly the way I looked when I stared at my reflection on January 1, 1923. On both occasions I said to myself "What do I do now?"

Well, here's what I did in 2023. I got on the internet, clicked on Travelocity and booked a flight and rental car to Miami. I wanted to visit Pedro. Why after all these years? I don't know. The spirits don't know. I just did.

I've actually gone to Calvary Cemetery in Tampa three or four times. In fact, I visited Pedro's grave just last month. I don't travel for anything else. Not for entertainment. Not for business. But Pedro... Well, I can still shed a tear over him, *amigos*, even though the last time we were together as lovers was over 100 years ago; even though he died as an old man decades ago while I've stayed young.

He was the lucky one.

My life is utterly empty. Over the course of one hundred years I have acquired every material thing I could ever want. But I have had no lover, no joy, no one to share my life with except these *cabrón* Tikal spirits whispering in my ears. One hundred years of nothing but me and the condominiums and office buildings I buy and sell through my don't-ask-don't-tell entourage of brokers and lawyers. Nothing but me sitting at the old wooden desk I rescued from that shithole apartment I lived in on Yucca and that I've retained since the Roaring 1920s. Picture me sitting at this old desk with a series of increasingly sophisticated typewriters – manual, then electric – and, now, computers that I write soulless entertainments on.

Soulless. Heartless. As if Buluc Chabtan and Ah Puch were my only audience. Well. No disrespect intended, *amigos*, but maybe they are. Waiting, always waiting to collect their due.

But maybe time is no longer patient enough to wait.

Amigos, before I end this story, let me tell you about my decision. Ever since I went to visit Pedro's grave in Florida this last time I've been wondering... what if I were to go back to Tikal and offer the Bleeding Stone this piece of gold in my chest that pretends to be a heart? Uncle Carlos had hinted about it back in Tikal – the words he said have never left me: "Now you can live as long as you like. Take of the world what you can get. And when you finally decide you've had enough, the gold comes back here." I remembered the pile of gold-shaped hearts in the Treasury room.

If I go back to Tikal and offer my heart to those old bastards of war and death, will I finally die?

I said these words out loud and, for only the third or fourth time in a hundred years, the *fantasmas* went completely silent. I take that as a yes. Maybe those parasites are as tired of me as I am of them.

Yes. It's time.

So, I'm going back to Tikal. It's a big tourist site now – one of Guatemala's great national parks. But I should have no trouble slipping in. I've seen pictures of the *Templo de los Muertos* on the internet. In fact, I've seen architectural studies of it on a Guatemalan university website. Not one archaeologist has yet discovered that there is a secret Shadow Room – a *Cuarto de Sombras* – under the main ceremonial hall. And I'm the only one alive who knows how to enter it. Well, I suppose it's possible that there may be one other who knows.

It's amazing. A greedy world like this one and nobody realizes that there's a king's ransom of gold and jade still hidden there. I figure that all I have to do is go to that pyramid of horrors and offer those hungry gods this gold rock in my chest. What will happen? After a few minutes of earthquakes and spirits screaming — lo and behold! – Ah Puch and Buluc Chabtan get to join their hellish bodies again fueled by yet another broken-ribbed skeleton in the pit. *Ay,* but with one important difference. Since I will do it willingly rather than as a victim, I won't become just another anguished Tikal voice. I'll finally be free.

Amigos, I have one other thing I have to tell you. When I said there may be one other…? Well, I don't think I'll be going to Tikal alone. Something happened today. You know by now that I like surfing the internet, right? Well, I was going through Facebook wondering if any of the people I was trolling might be undead like me. And there was a sudden ping on the computer. It was a friend request.

From an *hombre* named Carlos Lopez of Antigua, Guatemala. I looked at the picture and the profile. Yes, *amigos*. It's my Uncle Carlos! I mean, Jesus! Carlos is still alive! A hundred years later and still looking like he's in his 30s. That can only mean one thing. Setting aside the vileness of our last interaction when he grabbed *mis privadas* and pressed those nasty lips to mine, I remembered him saying that now we were brothers. I remembered how he'd never remove his clothes to bathe in the river or sleep. He rarely removed his shades. True, when I drank the elixir and lay paralyzed on the Bleeding Stone I saw him in nothing but a loincloth in the shadow of strange firelight. But his body was covered in indigo paint, so who could say if it was tinged gold? But without question I remember the visions I had of the scars on his chest. The same massive scars that I see everyday in the bathroom mirror. Well, shit. Ah Puch and Buluc Chabtan really get around.

I had to laugh. But bitterly, you know? Catrina was right. She told me that that *cabrón* would never die. Well, let that be his decision. My *Tío* Carlos! And he called *me* a *pendejo!* His very memory pisses me off. I hope he's been as tormented as me. I'm guessing that he's finally tortured enough to give up the ghost. Why else would he contact me?

And so, *amigos*, I shall accept his gracious friend request. Then I shall tell him what I plan to do. I'll stop in Antigua on my way to Tikal. I'll pick him up and we'll drive the whole way to the *Templo de los*

Muertos in an air-conditioned Mercedes Benz rented from Hertz Car Rental in Guatemala City.

To give up the ghost.... That raises a question I've been afraid to ask myself for the last hundred years. Do *hombres* like me – men who have no heart – do we still have souls? I'm serious. I can't ask a priest and I don't know who else might have an answer to that. *Amigos,* maybe you know how to answer that one. Think about it for me, will you?

As for all of my wealth – the gold, the real estate, the royalties. I will talk to my lawyers before I leave. Pedro Luna's grandchildren and great-grandchildren are going to get one helluva surprise from a great-uncle they never knew they had.

My final words are for Pedro. What you said about me not having a heart – I'm glad now that you know it wasn't true. I loved you. I still do. I want my human heart back even if it's shriveled dead and turned to dust these last hundred years. I want it back. Maybe then this body can finally sleep. And maybe – if my years of purgatory are done – this lost spirit will finally get to see you on the other side.

The End